THE WICKED CAT

Don't miss any of the chilling adventures!

SPOOKSVILLE

THE WICKED CAT

Christopher Pike

Aladdin

NEW YORK   LONDON   TORONTO   SYDNEY   NEW DELHI

ALADDIN

An imprint of Simon & Schuster Children's Publishing Division
1230 Avenue of the Americas, New York, NY 10020
This Aladdin edition October 2015
Text copyright © 1996 by Christopher Pike
Jacket illustration copyright © 2015 by Vivienne To
Also available in an Aladdin paperback edition.
All rights reserved, including the right of reproduction
in whole or in part in any form.
ALADDIN is a trademark of Simon & Schuster, Inc.,
and related logo is a registered trademark of Simon & Schuster, Inc.
For information about special discounts for bulk purchases,
please contact Simon & Schuster Special Sales at 1-866-506-1949
or business@simonandschuster.com.
The Simon & Schuster Speakers Bureau can bring authors to your live event.
For more information or to book an event contact the Simon & Schuster Speakers
Bureau at 1-866-248-3049 or visit our website at www.simonspeakers.com.
Jacket designed by Jessica Handelman
Interior designed by Mike Rosamilia
The text of this book was set in Weiss Std.
Manufactured in the United States of America 0915 FFG
2 4 6 8 10 9 7 5 3 1
Library of Congress Control Number 2014950418
ISBN 978-1-4814-1087-8 (hc)
ISBN 978-1-4814-1086-1 (pbk)
ISBN 978-1-4814-1088-5 (eBook)

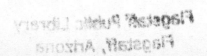

1

THE BLACK CAT WAS WAITING FOR THEM ON the path.

They weren't far outside of town when they bumped into it. Lately, because they'd been running into so much trouble in the woods and hills surrounding Spooksville, they had stayed closer to town. Actually, a lot of days they never even left the city. The whole summer they'd had adventure after adventure, and even though they'd enjoyed most of them—after they were over—they felt that each adventure was making them old before their time. Watch especially had gotten tired of risking his life, and said he had a new goal—to live long enough to get his driver's license.

"They'll never give you a driver's license," Sally Wilcox said as they walked on a path just east of the cemetery, which wasn't a bad spot if you liked glorious views of a witch's castle and tons of tombstones. Spooksville had a much higher death rate than birth rate. Sally brushed aside her dark bangs and continued, "You can't see well enough to pass the eye test."

"I've thought of that," Watch, who seemed to have been born without a last name, said. He always wore four watches—two on an arm, each set for a different time zone in the country. "But I plan to memorize the chart beforehand."

"That would be cheating," Cindy Makey, always one to be worried about what was right and proper, said. She had long blond hair and was very pretty.

"The means justify the end," Watch said.

"But you might still have trouble driving," Adam Freeman reminded him gently. Adam, who usually led the group, was short with dark hair. He worried about his height and doing the right thing. "If you can't see the road and all."

"Yeah, you might run over little kids like old Harry Hit and Run," Sally said.

"I won't be like him," Watch said.

"Why? What did he do?" Cindy asked.

"His name sort of explains it all, don't you think?" Sally replied, always trying to put Cindy down.

"He was an old guy who used to drive around in a boat-size black Cadillac and tried to run kids over," Watch said. "If you saw him coming, you had to get out of his way. He didn't care if you were on the sidewalk or not, he'd speed up and try to hit you."

"Did he ever kill anyone?" Adam asked, horrified.

"Dozens," Sally answered solemnly.

"I can't remember anyone specific," Watch corrected. "But he sure tried his best all the time. One day his nastiness got the best of him. He ran into a telephone pole and when it fell down on him, he was electrocuted."

"The kids in town didn't want him buried," Sally said. "We all signed a petition to hang him on the town Christmas tree that year. He glowed in the dark and actually looked better dead than alive."

Cindy shook her head. "I can't believe you hung a corpse on a Christmas tree."

"Wait till you see some of the Christmas presents people give each other in this town," Sally said wisely. "Then you'll see that a corpse is nothing."

"What happened to Harry's Cadillac?" Adam asked.

"It seems Harry had possessed it," Watch said. "It drove down to Hollywood and tried to get bit parts in horror films. I've seen it in a few movies that went straight to video. It got itself a new paint job and is now bright red."

"A car can't be possessed," Cindy said, annoyed.

"If kids with good grades can be possessed," Sally said, "a car can be."

It was just then that they noticed the cat sitting on the path in front of them.

What impressed Adam most about it was how shiny its black fur was. The cat looked groomed by a professional. Also, it had intense green eyes that glowed as bright as any Christmas light. As it stared at them, Adam felt as if he were being examined from the inside out. To be quite honest, he took an immediate dislike to the cat. But he didn't say that to the others because it sounded stupid to take a personal dislike to an animal. Especially when Sally seemed so taken with it.

"Wow," Sally said, stopping them. "Look at that cat. It looks like a princess or something the way it's sitting there."

"But it's a black cat," Cindy said. "Isn't it supposed to be unlucky to have a black cat cross your path?"

"That's just superstition," Adam answered her.

"But since every other superstition in the book seems to be true in Spooksville we might want to watch it," Watch said.

"Nonsense," Sally replied. "It's a beautiful cat. Look at the way it's watching us. And it doesn't have a collar. Maybe it's a stray and doesn't belong to anyone."

"You know you don't have a good history with the things you find to take home," Watch said, referring to the Wishing Stone, which had almost got all of them stranded on a slave planet for the rest of their miserable lives.

"A cat can't be dangerous," Sally said. "Look, I think she likes me."

"You suffer from a strange belief that everyone likes you," Cindy muttered.

Sally took a step forward. "Here kitty, kitty, kitty. Come to Sally."

It seemed Sally was right. The cat immediately walked over and licked Sally's hands as she knelt to greet it. Watch leaned over and spoke to Adam.

"I think it must be a very tolerant cat," he said.

"I heard that," Sally muttered. "Any of you guys got any food on you?"

"Like I always carry a can of tuna in my back pocket," Cindy said.

Adam stepped to Sally's side. "It looks like it's well fed," he said, "so it must belong to someone."

"Then how come it doesn't have a collar on?" Sally asked.

"You don't wear a collar and you belong to some-one," Watch said.

"I'm trying to help out a stray animal here," Sally said. "Why are you guys giving me such a hard time?"

"We're just jealous that the cat likes you and doesn't like us," Cindy said sarcastically.

The cat stared at her with its bright green eyes and Sally smiled.

"Animals can see the inner person," Sally said. "They don't judge people by exterior traits."

"This cat must be as blind as me," Watch said.

"If you take it home with you and feed it," Adam warned Sally, "you might have trouble getting rid of it."

Sally stood with the cat snuggled in her arms. Actu-ally, it was sort of a big cat to carry. Adam couldn't help noticing how sharp its claws were. He was more of a dog person himself. He'd had to leave his dog in Kansas City when they moved from there to Spooksville. He still missed Lucky, who had been a sweet old mutt.

"Why should I want to get rid of it?" Sally asked.

"Your parents might not want it," Cindy said.

"But if I scream just right and throw a fit they'll warm to it," Sally said.

"I'm still worried it might belong to someone else," Adam said. "The owner could be hiking somewhere out here, not far from us. Why don't you put the cat down and see if it decides to follow us?"

Sally hesitated. "That won't prove anything."

"I know," Adam said, "but at least that way you'll get an idea if it has another master."

Sally reluctantly set the cat down. "All right. But if a big wolf comes along and eats it after we leave here I will hold you personally responsible, Adam."

"There are no wolves in Spooksville," Cindy said.

"Wait till the next full moon," Watch said. "Hike deep enough into the forest and you'll see a few of those nonexistent wolves turn into people."

"Let's get back," Adam said. "I need some ice cream."

They started back down the path. The cat took no time making its intentions clear. It followed them and Sally was delighted.

At least none of them had to carry it, Adam thought. He was worried about picking up any stray animal. It could have rabies, or worse.

Back in town they went to the Frozen Cow, the only ice-cream place in town, where only vanilla was served. Lately, though, they'd convinced the owner to put chocolate syrup on their ice cream so they could have a little variety. Each of them ordered a dish with two scoops and plenty of syrup. They had just sat down to eat when the cat jumped up on the table and tried to lick Cindy's dish. Before the animal could get to it, though, Cindy shoved it off the table.

"Hey!" Sally said. "Don't be so rough."

"An animal shouldn't be up on a table," Cindy said.

The cat didn't seem to agree.

Right then Cindy let out a howl of pain.

The cat had scratched Cindy's lower leg. Scratched it bad, Adam noticed. Cindy was already bleeding from four distinct lines. Cindy started to kick the cat away when Sally jumped up to stop her.

"You started it," Sally said. "You hurt it first."

"I didn't hurt it," Cindy protested. "I just pushed it out of the way."

"That's exactly what Hitler said about Poland at the start of World War Two," Watch remarked.

"I'm bleeding," Cindy went on. "And that cat is responsible. Get it out of here."

Sally reached down and picked up the cat. But not to get rid of it. "No," she said. "Animals have rights, too. I think you should apologize to the cat, Cindy."

Cindy snorted and picked up a white napkin to wipe her leg. "Like it would understand me," she snapped.

Sally scratched the top of the cat's head. "Cats are some of the smartest animals there are. They are descended from lions."

"And we all know how popular those are in Disney films," Watch remarked under his breath.

They returned to eating their ice cream, while Cindy simmered and Sally spoon-fed the cat half her dish. The cat enjoyed the vanilla ice cream, but not the chocolate syrup. When they were finished, Cindy angrily left to go home for a bandage. Watch and Adam followed Sally home. The cat was sticking close to Sally now, never moving more than a foot from her legs. Sally seemed to enjoy the attention.

"Can you believe that Cindy?" Sally said. "She is so insensitive. She could have broken the cat's neck shoving it like that."

"I suspect this cat could jump off a three-story building and not get hurt," Watch said.

"Cindy got a pretty nasty scratch," Adam said. "Cuts like that can be dangerous. I don't think you can blame Cindy for getting upset."

Sally was annoyed. "Why do you always take her side?"

"Maybe he does so because your side usually lands us in a situation where we almost get killed," Watch said.

"I don't always take her side," Adam replied. "I just think you act rashly sometimes, is all."

Sally snorted. "I am spontaneous, not rash. There's a difference."

2

Sally's parents weren't home, but the guys stayed anyway and played chess. Actually, Sally and Adam played together as a team against Watch, who was extremely good at the game. When Watch managed to take their queen only twenty moves into the game, Sally scowled.

"How can we beat this guy?" she asked. "He practices every night against his computer."

"I know this sounds weird but my computer refuses to play with me anymore," Watch said.

"Your computer is a machine," Adam said, trying to figure out how to save the game. "How can it refuse you anything?"

"Ordinarily I would agree with you," Watch said. "But the last time I tried to play chess against my computer it took software from a *Star Trek* game I have and fired phasers at both my king and queen. The computer didn't want checkmate, it wanted total annihilation." Watch paused. "I'll have you guys checkmated in three moves."

"How do you know what moves we're going to make?" Sally asked.

"You always make the same mistakes," Watch said.

Just then they heard a loud crash and a painful yelp. Sally jumped up. "Where's the cat?"

"You said you put it in the backyard," Adam said, also hopping up.

"Let's take a look," Sally said.

In the backyard they found that the neighbor's tree had fallen down and apparently struck the neighbor's dog, a golden retriever, who had been barking a few minutes earlier. The dog was limping now, clearly in pain. But since the neighbor's yard was separated from them by a white picket fence, they weren't sure what to do.

"Is your neighbor home?" Adam asked Sally.

"No," she said. "Mr. Coat works long hours at an oil refinery north of town. He gets home after dark."

The dog continued to yelp.

"We have to help the poor thing," Adam said. "I think we should climb the fence."

"How can you help it?" Sally asked. "What are you going to do, give it a doggie biscuit?"

"We see that her love of all little furry creatures doesn't extend to animals that don't get along with cats," Watch remarked.

Sally looked worried. "Where is my cat?"

They found it on the far side of the house, licking its paws and yawning. Sally picked it up and carried it to the back porch. "Poor kitty," she cooed. "Was that big bad dog barking at you?"

But Adam continued to worry about the dog.

"I think the falling tree might have broken its leg," he said. "I'm going to climb the fence to check."

"Mr. Coat doesn't like people on his property," Sally warned. "He once sprayed a bunch of trick-or-treaters with gasoline and tried to set them on fire."

"That was water because the trick-or-treaters were trying to light his house on fire," Watch corrected.

"What's the difference?" Sally asked.

Adam climbed over the fence, a tricky maneuver because of the sharp pickets. For a moment he slipped and almost stuck himself bad. But soon he was in Coat's yard. The golden retriever seemed friendly enough, and immediately limped over to Adam to lick his hand. Adam studied the dog's hind leg. It had been a large pine tree that had obviously hit the poor animal. Yet even though the animal squirmed as Adam ran his fingers along the dog's leg, Adam was soon convinced nothing was broken.

He called out to the others, "I think he just got bruised."

"Serves him right for barking at kitty," Sally said.

"Oh, that's really fair," Watch said with sarcasm. "All dogs should be punished for barking. And every police officer should be abused for writing parking tickets. And every politician should be arrested for making promises he can't keep. And—"

"You've made your point," Sally interrupted.

"I wish I had a dog like this," Adam said. He was just about to climb back over the fence when something odd about the fallen tree caught his eye. Walking over to it, he noticed that the point where it had cracked and fallen was scorched black. He told the others and Watch was intrigued.

"Is there a downed electrical wire nearby?" he asked.

"A tree wouldn't fall down because you electrocuted it," Sally said.

"Then how did it fall?" Watch asked her.

Sally shrugged. "The wind."

"But there isn't any wind today," Watch said.

"You're such a stickler for details," Sally said, still stroking the cat.

Adam reached down and touched the black bark. It was warm.

"I'd like you to come over here," he said. "This is weird."

"You go," Sally said to Watch as she stepped up on the porch. "I think kitty wants dinner."

Watch managed to climb the fence and soon was standing beside the fallen tree, studying the burnt wood. The black marks cut almost to the core of the trunk. Yet there was something peculiar about that as well.

"Notice that the burn only radiates from one side," Watch said, pointing. "It doesn't go all the way around."

"What could cause that?" Adam asked.

"A lightning strike; it would have to be from the direction of Sally's house."

"But there isn't a cloud in the sky," Adam protested.

Watch nodded, puzzled. "But I can't think of anything else that would burn a tree like this. The burn definitely has to be the reason it fell down, and since the rest of the tree didn't catch fire, I suspect it got struck all at once and quickly."

"It looks like it was struck with a laser blast," Adam said.

"Yeah," Watch agreed. "But I gave this planet's only laser pistol back to the Kaster admiral on Amacron Thirty-seven. You remember?"

"Yeah," Adam said thoughtfully. "You know what's also strange about this tree? That it managed to fall on the dog."

Watch nodded. "Yeah. It's like someone timed it to hurt the poor guy."

"But what or who would do such a thing?"

Watch smiled. "Sally, if you gave her half the chance. Come on, let's go inside. We still have to finish our game."

"Just don't go lasering my king," Adam said.

3

LATER THE THREE OF THEM REJOINED Cindy and decided to go see a movie. Sally left the cat at home with a note to her parents explaining that either the cat stayed or their daughter was moving.

There was only one movie theater in Spooksville and it rarely showed anything but horror films, which was okay with the gang because the films were pretty tame compared to their own lives. They had just settled down with popcorn and drinks to watch a film about vampires who were spreading across the world disguised as used car salesmen when the cat appeared in the aisle and started meowing for Sally's attention. They were pretty amazed that the cat had not only followed them to the theater, but had managed to sneak in as well.

"It really loves me," Sally said, pleased at the interruption. She picked up the cat and offered it some popcorn. The cat wasn't interested.

"We can't watch a movie with a cat," Cindy said.

"Why not?" Sally snapped.

"It's against the rules to bring a cat into the theater," Cindy said. "Besides it might scratch me again."

"It won't hurt you unless you abuse it again," Sally said.

Adam sighed. "Are we going to get to watch this movie or not?"

"I know I would enjoy it more if the two female vampires beside us would stop fighting," Watch said.

But Sally and Cindy couldn't stop arguing—or refused to stop—so the guys decided they'd be better off if they all left and came back to see the movie later. Leaving the theater with their buckets of popcorn, they headed for Cindy's. But Cindy, of course, wouldn't let the cat in the house.

"My mother is allergic to cats," Cindy said. "Even a little cat hair makes her eyes swell up."

"I think you just invented that," Sally said, holding on to the cat. "What if I tell you that if she doesn't go in, I don't go in?"

"You don't exactly have a lot of leverage in that statement," Watch said.

"Why don't you just come in for a little while?" Adam suggested, always trying to compromise. "The cat seems to like you a lot. It should wait for you on the porch."

"All right," Sally said reluctantly, "but we have to feed her soon."

"She can have a peanut butter and jelly sandwich. That's all we have," Cindy said, going inside.

They were in the middle of making the cat a sandwich when they smelled smoke. At first Cindy thought something was burning in the kitchen. But then they all realized the smell was coming from the front of the house. Peeking out the front door, they were horrified to see the porch was on fire!

"I'll get the hose by the garage!" Adam shouted. "Watch, you get the other one in the backyard! Sally, Cindy, try to smother the flames with an old blanket or sheet!"

The porch was old and made of wood, very dry wood after a whole summer of hot days—perfect burning material. But even though the flames were growing and licking the roof of the porch, none of the house proper had been touched. The girls beat at the flames with blankets while Adam turned on the garage hose.

The water pressure was excellent, and two minutes after turning the hose on the flames, the fire was out. When Watch returned from the backyard with the other hose, he insisted they water down the entire roof.

"You never know," he said. "A cinder may have flown up and it could be smoldering, ready to ignite."

The porch was badly damaged, and Cindy stared at it in horror. "My mother's going to kill me," she said.

"But you didn't do anything," Adam said. "In fact, if we hadn't been here the fire might have taken out the whole house."

"Yeah," Sally agreed. "Spooksville's fire department sure wouldn't have been able to put it out. If you have a fire in this town you have to fill out six different forms and get each one notarized before they'll come out. They're so paranoid about getting sued."

"But I was here when the fire started," Cindy said. "It has to be my fault."

"I don't know about that," Watch muttered. "This is the second fire we've seen today."

"What second fire?" Sally asked. "There was no fire at Mr. Coat's house."

Adam and Watch hadn't mentioned the strange black marks on the tree. But they did now and Cindy became immediately suspicious.

"It's too much of a coincidence that these two things should happen in the same day," Cindy said.

"What are you saying?" Sally demanded.

"At both places where there was a fire the black cat was nearby," Cindy said.

Sally snorted. "How can a cat start a fire?"

"The fire that knocked the tree down was not an ordinary fire," Watch said. "It looked as if the tree had been blasted by an energy beam. I suggest we study the porch to see if it has similar markings."

"That would be a waste of time," Sally protested.

"We have time," Adam said.

But it wasn't as easy to examine the porch as the tree since so much of it had been burned. They weren't even sure what part of the porch had started burning first. But after a time Watch found a spot down near the steps where he thought it had begun. He pointed out a set of four black lines, each one an inch thick and separated from the next one by a couple of inches.

"It looks to me like someone carefully swept this spot with whatever they were using," he said.

"That makes sense," Sally said. "With 'whatever they were using.' *What* were they using and who were *they?*"

Watch frowned. "These marks could have been created by a blowtorch, maybe. No, actually they look too neat. They remind me of marks left by a laser beam. What do you think, Adam?"

Adam nodded. "It does look like the fire was deliberately started. No one saw anybody hanging around the house?"

"There was just the cat," Cindy said angrily.

"And how, my dear, did the cat start the fire?" Sally asked. "I don't think it's old enough to smoke."

"It's bad luck," Cindy snapped. "I'd be a lot happier if you got rid of it."

"Fortunately my main goal in life is not your happiness," Sally said.

"Where is the cat anyway?" Adam asked.

"Here it comes," Sally said, as the cat came from around the side of the house, right on cue. Sally knelt to allow the cat to run into her arms, which the animal promptly did. Sally smiled and stroked the cat's back while the animal purred appreciatively. Its eyes never left Cindy, who continued to worry about the damage done to her porch.

"I don't like the way it looks at me," Cindy said.

"You should be pleased she even bothers," Sally said.

"Sally," Adam said diplomatically, "why don't you take the cat home and we'll see you tomorrow? It's getting late."

Sally pouted. "I get it. Either I get rid of the cat or I'm no longer your friend. Well, to tell you the truth, I don't need friends who hate an animal just because it has four legs. You know, Adam, at one time I thought we'd be friends for the rest of our lives. But now I see that you're just a—"

"Sally," Adam interrupted gently. "The situation is not that serious. Cindy is just upset about what's happened here and you are making everything worse by taunting her."

Sally stuck her nose in the air. "All right. I can take a hint. I know when I'm not wanted. I'll go home now, and if I don't happen to run into you guys for a few months, then that's life. None of us should be upset at the lack of contact. I wish you all well. I harbor no ill feelings."

And with that Sally walked away, her cat in her hands.

"Isn't it wonderful she was so mature about the whole thing?" Watch muttered.

"What am I going to do about the porch?" Cindy asked miserably.

Adam patted her on the back. "I think you'd better find your mother and brother so you can tell her what's happened. She'll understand, and Watch and I will back you up and say that we weren't playing with fire or anything dangerous like that."

"All right," Cindy said. She went into the house to call her mom at a friend's. Watch knelt once more to study the burn marks. Adam stood behind his shoulder.

"It's possible the fire was started by a welding gun," Watch said.

"Who do we know who has one?" Adam asked.

Watch stood. "That may not be the main issue. Let's think about what happened today. We found the cat and we took it to the Frozen Cow. But when Cindy pushed it out of the way, she ended up with several nasty scratches. Next we went to Sally's house. We left the cat in her backyard where the dog next door started to bark at it. Then a tree just happened to fall on that dog. Finally we brought the cat here, but Cindy wouldn't let it in her house. And by a strange coincidence Cindy's house caught on fire." He paused. "Do you see a pattern here?"

"But you can't agree with Cindy that the cat was responsible for both fires," Adam said. "That just doesn't make sense."

"I don't know how it could have started them either. But I do know that cat doesn't like to be pushed around or annoyed. It has a nasty temper and seems fully capable of taking care of itself."

Adam was concerned. "Should we tell Sally these things? It might be dangerous for her to keep it. For all we know she might let it stay in the house with her tonight."

Watch considered. "Whatever we tell Sally right now won't do much good. She's obsessed with that cat. Let's wait and see what happens next."

Adam continued to worry. "You know, I never knew Sally was so into cats."

"She never was."

Adam looked at Watch. "Are you saying the cat might be responsible for Sally's obsession with it? That it has her hypnotized?"

Watch shrugged. "I don't know. Those are pretty far-out ideas. We might be making a fuss about nothing." He added, "All I know is, that cat gives me the creeps."

Adam didn't respond.

He had felt the same way the moment he had seen the cat.

4

THAT EVENING SALLY WATCHED TV ALONE in her room. She had acted annoyed with her friends for not liking her cat, but the truth was she really was hurt. Sally seldom got really excited about anything, but the cat did mean a lot to her. She couldn't understand how they could think the cat was responsible for a tree falling and a porch burning. Cindy especially was unreasonable. Whenever anything went wrong Cindy was always quick to come up with the most ridiculous idea why it was wrong. Sally didn't understand why Cindy couldn't be more logical—like herself.

But Sally was a little worried that she might not see

her friends—and that included Cindy—for a few days. There weren't that many days left of the summer, and she didn't want to waste them being all alone. Sally hated to be alone, especially with a stupid TV set. She couldn't believe the programs they put on these days. Why, even the shows that were supposed to be scary didn't deal with half the issues she had to deal with just living in Spooksville. What was so scary about an alien invasion? She and her friends had repulsed several alien attacks, all by themselves. Network executives just didn't understand what kids could do.

"Come here, kitty," Sally called to the cat, which had been sitting on the floor by her bed, staring at the TV with her. Actually, the cat seemed to be following the programs, and once again Sally congratulated herself on finding such a smart cat. The animal jumped on her bed at her call and snuggled up against her. Sally liked having something to love. In a way, she thought, it was nicer than always having to be so insulting. Sometimes she got tired of her own insults, but that was not something she'd ever tell anybody.

"Nice kitty," she said, thinking she'd have to think up a name for it soon if she was going to keep it. But she worried that the real owners were going to show up soon. Like Adam said, a cat as beautiful and well groomed as this couldn't have been running in the wild for long. "Beautiful kitty," she said.

The cat stared up at her. It had such incredible green eyes, Sally thought. They actually seemed to glow. And when she stared at them, it was as if nothing else mattered. They were so soothing and loving. Sally thought the cat must have the soul of an angel. She decided right then that she'd let the cat sleep in the house tonight. No way she was going to let that stupid dog next door bark at it again. In fact, Sally thought, she would let the cat sleep on her bed.

Sally had heard the old superstition that sleeping with a cat could be dangerous because the animal could actually suck the life out of one's body. Sally thought the superstition was stupid. Cats were much smarter and nicer than dogs, and so much cleaner. If the cat wanted to sleep on the pillow beside her, that was all right with Sally.

Sally suddenly felt sleepy. Turning off the TV, she got ready for bed, brushing her teeth and putting on her pajamas. In a few minutes she was tucked in, with the kitty resting beside her. Usually Sally's mind was so active, it took her at least half an hour to unwind so she could sleep. But tonight she found herself drifting off within a few seconds.

And she dreamed. It was such a vivid dream, and so strange. She was walking in Spooksville late at night but it was a much different Spooksville from the one she knew. It was as if she'd been transported back in time two hundred years earlier. There were far fewer buildings and the ones that did exist were built of large gray stones. Yet she knew it was Spooksville because she recognized the coastline and the surrounding hills and mountains. Even in the dark, she was able to see far off.

But Sally wasn't just walking aimlessly. She had an appointment to keep with a friend, Madeline Templeton, who was a young girl like herself, but also a witch with mysterious powers. Madeline was to meet her at the cemetery. Sally knew she would recognize her because she was her friend—of course—and because she looked like the present-day Ann Templeton.

For Sally, it was as if the two time frames had overlapped. She had memories of the past and the future. She was definitely Sally Wilcox, but she was also someone else as well. She was meeting with Madeline because Madeline had promised to share some of her power in exchange for a small favor. Sally didn't know what this "small favor" was, but whatever it was she had already made up her mind to do it. She didn't like being ordinary. She wanted power to make things happen.

She saw the cemetery, the dark tombstones.

The wind blew and leaves danced.

She saw Madeline approaching.

Madeline's eyes were so very green and bright, like a cat's.

Then Sally woke up and her own cat was staring at her.

Sally thought she was awake. Her eyes were open. Yet she couldn't move her body; it was so heavy it felt made of stone. Plus the cat's eyes were so big that when Sally tried to turn her head, she couldn't. She suspected that even if she could, she would still see the cat's eyes. They seemed to fill the room. The cat licked its white teeth with its pink tongue. Then it spoke to her without saying anything aloud. There was a peculiar quality to the telepathic voice. It hissed and crooned, as a cat's voice might. It spoke to her as if it were wiser and older than she.

"You know who I am?" it asked.

Sally heard her own voice respond. It seemed as if she heard it from a thousand miles away. "You are my cat."

"I am much more than a cat. I am a powerful magician."

"Oh. Then why do you look like a cat?"

"That's because I choose to look like one. But I can look any way I wish."

"Could you look like a lion?"

"Yes. I could look like a lion or the most beautiful girl in the world. Would you like such power?"

"Sure."

"I can give it to you. I can give you all you wish."

"Really?"

"Yes. You believe me, don't you?"

"I suppose. Did you set Cindy's porch on fire?"

"Yes. She was mean to me. She was lucky I did not set her on fire."

"Don't do that."

"Why not? I do what I wish. Are you sure you would like my power?"

Sally hesitated. There was something not quite right, but she couldn't figure out what it was. She just wished she could totally wake up. She still felt as if half her mind were dreaming. Yet the things the cat was saying were very interesting. It would be nice to work spells and magic.

"I would like your power," Sally mumbled. "I just don't want to hurt anyone."

"You can do what you want with the power. It is up to you. Would you like me to tell you the secret of how you can have it?"

"Yes."

"All you have to do is take hold of my front paws, and stare deep into my eyes, and wish you were a cat."

"But I don't want to be a cat."

"*That doesn't matter. You just have to pretend you want to be one. Here, take my paws, one in each of your hands.*"

Sally did as she was told.

"*Now look deep into my eyes and repeat to yourself again and again, 'I want to be a cat. Sally wants to be a cat. I want to be a cat.' Just keep saying that to yourself and keep staring at my eyes and soon you will have all the power that I do. 'Sally wants to be a cat Sally wants to be a cat.'*"

"I want to be a cat," Sally whispered. "Sally wants to be a cat."

Sally suddenly felt dizzy.

"*Don't stop! 'I want to be a cat. Sally wants to be a cat.'*"

Sally felt very strange. But she wanted those powers.

"I want to be a cat," she kept saying.

And the cat's green eyes kept growing larger and larger.

5

THE NEXT DAY THREE-QUARTERS OF THE gang—Adam, Cindy, and Watch—were having milk and doughnuts at their favorite coffee shop. The main topic was Sally, naturally—whether she was going to show up and whether she'd have her cat with her. Cindy didn't think so but Adam and Watch were optimistic.

"Sally gets bored when she's alone," Watch said. "She begins to talk to herself."

"She does that when she's around people," Cindy said.

"Maybe I shouldn't have told her to take her cat home," Adam said.

"She should just get rid of it," Cindy said. "It gives me a weird feeling."

Adam and Watch had not discussed all their fears with Cindy, worried they might scare her unnecessarily. Also, they didn't want her more mad at Sally than normal.

"I don't think she's going to part with that cat any time soon," Watch said.

"We have to get used to it," Adam agreed. "Maybe it's not so bad."

"Yeah," Cindy said sarcastically. "It will be perfect to have around at Halloween."

Just then a pretty girl about their age walked by the coffee shop. She waved to them through the window as if she knew them. Her black hair was long and very thick. Smiling, she pointed to the front door of the coffee shop as if asking whether she should join them. Adam and his friends didn't know what to do so they just nodded. The girl headed for the entrance.

"Who's that?" Adam asked.

"I've never seen her before," Watch said.

"She must be new in town," Cindy said.

"Yeah," Adam agreed. "But she acts like she knows us. Oh, here she comes."

"She has incredible hair," Cindy observed.

The girl came over to their table and without asking permission sat down. Her smile was dazzling; she had very bright white teeth. Her green eyes were unique; they seemed to glow. She was dressed in a pair of blue shorts and a white blouse that looked vaguely familiar. Her hands were also striking; she had the longest nails. She looked at each of them as if they should recognize her but none of them knew what to say to her. Finally she laughed.

"My name is Jessie," she said. "I used to live here. Now I live here again."

"Welcome back," Adam said carefully. "Did you just get into town?"

"Late last night," Jessie said. Her smile seemed frozen on her face.

"Where are you living?" Cindy asked.

Jessie shrugged. "Around. What are you guys up to today?"

"We're waiting for our friend Sally before we decide," Watch said.

Jessie brushed her hand. "I ran into Sally on the way over here. She said to tell you she wouldn't be seeing you for a while. She's still angry about yesterday."

"I knew it," Cindy muttered. "I get my leg scratched and my porch all burned and she's the one who gets mad."

Adam frowned. "Do you know Sally?"

"Yes. I know her from way back." Jessie licked her fingers and reached for a menu. "I hope this place has some decent food. I'm starving."

"I've never heard Sally mention you before," Watch said.

"So?" Jessie said as she studied the menu. "Hey, do you guys know if you can get a fish sandwich this early?"

"I think that's on the lunch menu," Adam said. "They just serve breakfast now. You can get eggs and bacon."

Jessie wrinkled her nose and her smile faltered. Once more she licked her fingers and then brushed her arms a few times.

"I'm a picky eater," she said. "Can I just get a bowl of milk?"

"You mean milk and cereal?" Cindy asked.

Jessie scowled. "No. I don't like cereal. I just want a bowl of milk."

"Why don't you get it in a glass?" Watch said.

"Fine." Jessie put down the menu and turned to Adam. "Could you order for me, Adam? I don't have any money."

"Sure."

Adam called the waitress over and asked for a glass of milk. While the woman went for it, Watch studied Jessie.

"What's your last name?" he asked.

She was offended. "What is this? An interrogation? I'm here to have fun. What do you guys want to do today?"

They stared uneasily around the table.

"As we said before we're still hoping Sally will show up," Adam said. "Then we'll decide."

"But as I told you she said she won't be showing up," Jessie snapped. Then she smiled suddenly, especially at Adam. "Why do you need her to have fun? I can take her place."

"She's our friend," Cindy said. "We like to include her in whatever we do."

Jessie frowned at Cindy. "She's not your friend. She doesn't even like you."

Cindy was offended. "You don't know that."

"Yes I do. She told me so."

Watch was skeptical. "She just passed you on the street and said, 'Hi, Jessie. How are you? You know I don't like Cindy Makey.'" Watch paused. "That doesn't sound like Sally."

Jessie spoke in a cold voice. "She told me she wanted to spend more time with her cat."

Adam looked at the others. "That sounds right. She said as much when we said good-bye yesterday."

"She was just upset," Cindy said. "She'll soon get bored with that ugly old cat."

Now Jessie was offended. She seemed to be very moody.

"Her cat is not ugly. Why, it is as nice as my cat."

"You have a cat, too?" Adam asked.

"Yes. It's waiting outside. I wouldn't bring it in."

"Sally would," Cindy muttered.

Jessie suddenly smiled. "My cat is brown. It won't cause the troubles Sally's cat did. It won't be able to."

Once more the gang exchanged looks.

Cindy asked, "What troubles did her cat cause?"

"We'll tell you our theory in a minute," Watch answered.

"How did you know Sally's cat was causing us trouble?" Adam asked.

Jessie brushed her arms again. "She told me. Hey, where's my milk?"

"It's coming," Adam said. "It takes a few minutes. Just be patient."

Jessie smiled. "You're kind of cute, Adam. Did anyone ever tell you that?"

"My m-mother," Adam stuttered.

Watch persisted. "So Sally passed you on the street and told you about our troubles with her cat?"

Jessie was defensive. "I already said that."

"What exactly did she say?" Watch asked.

"That you thought the cat used magical powers to knock down the tree and set Cindy's porch on fire," Jessie explained impatiently.

Adam frowned. "That doesn't sound like Sally."

"Why do you keep calling me a liar?" Jessie demanded.

"I didn't call you a liar," Adam protested.

"You implied that I was one," Jessie said.

Jessie's glass of milk finally arrived. But Jessie just stared at it before speaking to the waitress. "Can I have an empty bowl?"

The waitress wanted to know what for. Jessie pounded the table.

"Just get me the bowl!" she shouted.

The waitress went for the bowl.

"You shouldn't shout in public," Cindy said. "It's rude."

"I can do whatever I want," Jessie said, fiddling with the napkin as if she had never seen one before. Then she broke into a grin again. "The town has really changed since I was last here."

"How has it changed?" Watch asked.

Jessie was amazed. "Why, there are so many cars and buildings and roads. There are all kinds of new things."

"How long ago did you live here?" Watch asked.

"It was a long time ago," Jessie said with a wicked smile.

"How long ago exactly?" Watch persisted.

Jessie was annoyed. "I don't have to answer your questions. I don't have to answer to anyone."

"What about your parents?" Cindy asked. "You have to do what they say."

Jessie shook her head. "They're dead."

"That's too bad," Adam said sympathetically.

Jessie didn't seem to care. "They died a long time ago."

6

JESSIE'S CAT WAS WAITING FOR THEM OUT-
side. It was brown, and except for its large size, it didn't
really resemble the cat Sally had found the previous day.
Also this cat had brown eyes, which made it seem more
human than scary.

Yet Jessie didn't seem to like her cat. One of the first
things she did as they started down the block was kick it
when it accidentally stepped in front of her.

"Hey!" Cindy shouted. "That wasn't very nice."

Jessie seemed surprised. "I didn't think you liked
cats."

"Whether I like them or not is beside the point,"
Cindy said. "I don't go around kicking them."

Jessie was annoyed. "Yeah, but you don't mind pushing them to the floor or making them wait outside."

"Did Sally tell you all this?" Adam asked, puzzled. It sounded as if Sally had told this perfect stranger every single detail of what had happened the previous day.

"Of course," Jessie snapped. "Listen, you guys, I want to know, what are we going to do for fun today?"

"We're going to the library," Watch said. "There we're going to study quantum physics and organic chemistry."

Jessie frowned. "That's boring."

"Nothing fascinates us more than intellectual pursuits," Watch said.

"Particularly after we've had milk and doughnuts," Cindy added.

Jessie was obviously bewildered. "Well, I'm going to have to hook up with you guys later." She turned away. "Come on, Sassy, let me find you a raw fish to munch on. I'll see you later, Adam."

The cat didn't move, which annoyed Jessie even more.

"Come on," Jessie said, getting ready to boot the cat. "Or you'll get another stiff kick."

Adam stepped in front of the cat. "You're not going to hurt this animal."

Jessie was frustrated. "Why do you like this cat and not Sally's cat?"

"This one isn't creepy," Cindy answered.

"Who are you calling creepy?" Jessie snapped.

Watch spoke very softly. "Sally's cat, not you."

Jessie turned away. "You guys are not nearly as much fun as I thought you would be," she said and took off, leaving her cat behind.

When Jessie was gone, Watch scratched his head and sighed.

"There is something very strange about that girl," he said.

"Sally must trust her," Cindy said. "She told Jessie everything about us."

"No," Adam corrected. "Just everything about yesterday."

Watch crouched and studied the new cat. "Isn't it funny that we should run into two interesting cats in the space of two days?" he asked.

"What's unusual about this one?" Adam asked.

"It's awfully big," Watch said. "And it has a strange master."

"But it doesn't like its master," Cindy pointed out.

"That's curious in itself," Watch said, scratching the cat on the top of its head. Then he stood and looked up and down the street. "I want to go to Sally's house."

"But she doesn't want to see us," Cindy said.

"Jessie said that," Watch replied. "But I think Jessie tells lies."

Adam nodded. "I didn't believe a word that girl said. We should check out Sally, see how she's getting on with her cat."

When they got to Sally's house, they found she wasn't home. They waited around for a while but she never showed up. They decided she might be down at the beach, which was one of her favorite places to hang out as long as you didn't ask her to get too close to the water. She still had a thing about all the sharks that were supposed to swim just off the shore of Spooksville.

But Sally wasn't at the beach either.

Bum was, though, busily feeding the pigeons.

Dressed as usual in shabby clothes and a four-day-old beard, he asked if they would buy him a turkey sandwich. Naturally they got him one, as well as a large Coke, potato chips, and a few chocolate-chip cookies. They sat with Bum not far from the jetty while he hungrily ate his sandwich. He even fed some of it to Jessie's cat, which devoured the bread as well as the turkey. Bum laughed at the cat.

"This is a funny girl," he said. "She likes bread as much as meat. Not many cats do. Give her one of these cookies. See if she eats it."

Watch gave the cat a cookie and the animal promptly ate it.

"She must be hungry," Cindy remarked.

Bum continued to stare at the cat. "Where did you get this cat?"

"It belongs to a new girl in town, Jessie," Adam said.

"But she says she's not really new," Watch added. "She used to live here."

"Describe her to me," Bum said. When Watch was finished, Bum shook his head. "No girl named Jessie who looks like that ever lived here. I know everybody who's lived here in the last sixty years."

"Then she even lied to us about that," Cindy said, disgusted.

"Watch," Adam said, "tell Bum about the cat Sally found yesterday."

"Before you do that," Bum said, "tell me where Sally is. I never see you guys apart anymore."

"We had kind of a fight yesterday," Adam said. "She's not speaking to us."

Bum smiled. "That may not be such a bad thing for a few days. It gives all of you a rest."

Watch described the cat to Bum, and then explained about the tree falling and the porch burning. Bum continued to eat while Watch spoke, yet Adam noticed he was paying close attention. When Watch was done, Bum sat still thinking for a long time.

"I would really like to have a look at that other cat," he said finally.

"When Sally shows up I'm sure she'll show it to you," Adam said.

Bum shook his head. "I don't know if Sally is going to show up any time soon."

Adam was stunned. "What do you mean? Do you think her cat has hurt her?"

"I don't think her cat is a cat at all," Bum said.

"It sounds as smart as a person and is able to knock down trees and set houses on fire."

"But the cat loved Sally," Cindy said, worried. "I can't see it hurting her."

"The cat did not love Sally," Bum said. "The cat was using Sally."

Watch nodded. "It wanted to get her alone. I think I understand what happened."

"I don't understand," Adam said. "Tell me."

"Watch this," Bum said, picking up the cat and carrying it over to the sand. There he set the cat down and said, "Write something. Use your paws."

"What is this?" Cindy gasped.

"Shh," Watch said. "Watch. This cat is smart, too."

"But how do you know?" Adam asked.

The cat pawed at the sand. A moment later they realized it had traced out a name. The letters were wobbly and widely spaced but there was no mistaking what the cat was trying to tell them. The word in the sand was

SALLY

Cindy frowned. "How can a cat spell? How can it write?"

At last Adam understood. "Because it's not a cat."

"Of course it's a cat," Cindy protested.

Watch shook his head. "This cat is Sally. The other cat turned her into this cat."

Cindy was shocked. "But where is the other cat?"

Bum put the final piece in the puzzle for her.

"The other cat is that new girl you just met," he said.

7

AFTER THEY HAD SLIGHTLY RECOVERED FROM the shock of the revelation, Adam turned to Watch.

"You knew?" he asked Watch.

"I suspected," Watch said. "But I couldn't believe what my head was telling me. But notice how much Jessie licked her fingers and brushed herself—just like a cat. And she wanted to drink her milk out of a bowl—just like a cat. She even looked a little like Sally's cat."

"She had the same green eyes!" Cindy exclaimed.

"Exactly," Watch said. "But the real question now is how did she become a cat in the first place? And how did she manage to turn Sally into a cat?"

"Obviously she transferred an evil spell of some

kind onto Sally," Bum said. "Which is why she was so friendly to Sally—when she was a cat. She needed Sally to become human again."

"I wonder how long this Jessie was a cat," Cindy said.

"It must have been a long time if I never met her as a girl," Bum said. "But I think I have an idea who changed her into a cat, and why. Witches often use cats as familiars."

Watch nodded. "That's right."

"What's a familiar?" Adam asked.

"A familiar is like a witch's power pack," Bum said. "They are like an extra battery when a witch wants to cast a particularly powerful spell. The witch is able to draw power from a living creature. A familiar doesn't have to be a cat, but cats are the most common form of familiars, particularly black cats. That's where the super-stition about black cats comes from."

"But you don't think Ann Templeton turned this Jessie into a cat, do you?" Adam asked. Personally he liked Ann Templeton, even though she was the town witch. She was very beautiful and always nice to him. Well, almost always—he had almost died the last two times he was in her castle.

"Not Ann Templeton," Bum said. "Remember, we think this Jessie was changed a long time ago. Also, I've never known Ann Templeton to employ a familiar. I don't think it's her style. But the witch who helped found this town, Madeline Templeton, often used familiars. They were one of the keys to her great power."

"But if Madeline Templeton turned Jessie into a cat, then that means she's hundreds of years old," Cindy protested.

"Familiars can live a long time," Bum said.

"Remember how Jessie said everything looked so different?" Watch said. "I think she is from a different time."

"So Madeline cursed Jessie and she became a cat?" Adam asked.

"I don't think it's that simple," Bum said. "I think you have to agree to the change."

"But who would agree to be a cat?" Cindy asked.

"Madeline might have phrased the offer in such a way that it sounded attractive," Bum said. "Or else she lied to the original Jessie. Sally, also, must have cooperated with the cat last night when it started to change her. But maybe Jessie was able to hypnotize her, I don't know. A familiar can be very powerful."

"But how do we reverse the spell?" Adam asked. "We can't leave Sally as a cat. She has to start school with us in a couple of weeks."

Cindy smiled. "But she is easier to handle as a cat."

The cat growled.

"I don't know," Bum said. "I'm a bum, not a witch. If I was you I would go talk to Ann Templeton. I happen to know she's in town this morning, buying new clothes at the Tomb."

"There's a clothes shop in town called the Tomb?" Cindy asked.

"It's pretty interesting," Watch said. "A few of the mannequins are actually preserved corpses. They look so lifelike."

"I've heard some of them do come back to life from time to time," Bum said. "Especially when Ann Templeton is around."

Cindy made a face. "I don't want to go there."

"You don't have to," Adam said. "Watch and I can take the cat to her. We'll catch up with you later."

"You can come with me," Bum said to Cindy. "I'm going bowling."

"But doesn't it cost money to bowl?" Cindy asked.

Bum smiled. "That's why I want you to come along."

Adam and Watch did find Ann Templeton at the Tomb. She was in the middle of getting some clothes altered and didn't appear to be happy about being interrupted. But when she saw the cat they had brought, she immediately took a break to talk to them. As always, with her long dark hair and bewitching eyes, she was beautiful. She

spoke to them in the reception area away from the mannequins and the weird shop owner, who was dressed like
a thirsty vampire with bad taste.

"Where did you get this cat?" Ann Templeton
demanded.

"We think it's Sally," Adam said. He then proceeded to
tell her the whole story. Ann Templeton listened closely.
When Adam was done, she picked up the cat and stared
deeply into its eyes. The animal growled at her but this
didn't seem to bother her. Finally she set the cat down.

"This is definitely your friend Sally," Ann Templeton said. "I remember Jessie now. She was a familiar of
my great-great-great-great grandmother's—Madeline
Templeton. They were childhood friends, actually, but
in the end I think Madeline must have been mad at her."

"Why?" Watch asked.

"Because she turned her into a cat," Ann Templeton
said simply. "You don't turn people you like into cats."

"That makes sense," Watch said.

"Can you turn Sally back into a person?" Adam asked.

"No," Ann Templeton said. "Not without the coopera-
tion of Jessie."

"But you are such a powerful witch," Watch said. "I
thought you could do anything."

Ann Templeton smiled. "Thank you, Watch. But

Madeline was more powerful than I am, and it was she who first set this spell in motion. The only way I can reverse it is if Jessie agrees to become a cat again." She paused. "But I think Sally is better off as a cat than as a human. She's less trouble."

"That's what Cindy said," Watch remarked.

"I know Sally," Adam said. "She probably hates being a cat. She can't talk, and that's pretty much all Sally ever does."

"Then you have to get Jessie to cooperate," Ann Templeton said.

"But she seems happy to be a human again," Watch said. "I don't think she's going to help us."

Ann Templeton stood. "You might try convincing her that being a human being isn't so great. She's been a cat for hundreds of years. I imagine the transition could be hard on her."

"But what if we can't convince her?" Adam asked.

Ann Templeton smiled. "Then that's your problem. Now if you will excuse me, I am being fitted for a new dress. Oh, how is your eyesight, Watch?"

"Better, ma'am," Watch said. "The blurring is gone. If I wear my glasses, I have no problem."

Ann Templeton was pleased. "You will go far, Watch, as will you, Adam. If this town doesn't kill you first. Good-bye."

"Good-bye," Adam and Watch said as she disappeared back into the depths of the Tomb. "At least she gave us some clues as to what to do," Watch said.

"I don't know," Adam said, depressed the witch hadn't just zapped Sally back into human form again. "What are we supposed to do next?"

"The question is what are *you* supposed to do next," Watch said. "You have to convince Jessie how lousy it is to be human."

"Why me?"

"Because she obviously likes you. But she doesn't like Cindy and me."

"She never said she likes me," Adam protested.

"She said you were cute; it's the same thing."

"But you said it yourself," Adam said. "She seems happy being human again."

"Yes. But she doesn't know how cruel our modern society can be. You have to point out to her the horrors of the twentieth century."

"How do I do that?" Adam asked.

"I don't know." Watch knelt and picked up the cat. "But you'll figure it out. Look, I'll take care of Sally and you take care of Jessie. Give me a call when Jessie is tired of being human."

"You might wait a long time for that call," Adam said gloomily.

8

AT THE ARCADE ADAM CAUGHT UP WITH Jessie, who was playing a game where she shot wolves that were trying to attack her. Adam stood and watched for a few minutes before speaking. He noticed that she just had to look at a machine to get to play another game. She didn't have to put in any quarters.

"She must still have magical powers," Adam said to himself. "I better be careful."

Adam walked over and said hello. She seemed happy to see him.

"Adam," she said. "Where are your annoying friends?"

"Oh, they're out doing stuff." He paused. "I was wondering if you wanted to spend the day with me?"

Her eyes widened and she turned away from the game. "That sounds like fun. What do you want to do?"

"We could go down to the school," he said. "You know it starts soon? You really should sign up."

She looked excited. "I haven't gone to school in a long time. What do I need to do to sign up?"

"You just have to write your name on some papers. We can buy a few of our books while we're there."

Jessie frowned. "You have to buy your own books?"

"Not most of them. Just a few. At least that's what Watch says. Come on, I have some extra cash."

They walked toward the school. Along the way Jessie almost got run over twice by cars.

"They come so fast," she complained. "I don't know how you stay out of their way."

"You have to watch the lights. You only go when they're green."

"I know that," Jessie said stiffly.

Adam had to sign up for school anyway. He'd been meaning to drop by for the last couple of days. They were sent to the gym, where some teachers were sitting behind tables. If you wanted to be in a teacher's class, you had to get in his or her line. They signed up for science, math, history, and English. For physical education Adam signed up for swimming, and put Jessie's name down as well. Jessie wasn't sure if she liked that choice.

"I don't know how to swim," she said.

"You'll learn," he said. "I'll give you a lesson this afternoon."

Jessie nodded but seemed uneasy.

Next they went to the book table. Adam really only had to buy one book but he bought a whole bunch to make it look as if school was harder than it was. He showed Jessie all the subjects they'd be studying.

"Algebra is hard," he said darkly. "You're going to have to study every night to keep up in that class."

Jessie was distressed. "But the last time I went to school all we did in math was add and subtract. Where did all this other stuff come from?"

"People invented it," Adam said. "And if someone invents something we all have to learn it. Let's go back to the coffee shop and have something to eat and I'll give you a few lessons."

Jessie was interested. "Can we get a fish sandwich?"

"We can try," Adam said.

But when they were seated in the coffee shop, Adam excused himself for a moment. He sneaked over and spoke to the waitress who was going to serve them. She was the same waitress they'd had that morning, and she looked at him a bit apprehensively. Big and fat, she wore tons of makeup and was chewing gum. Her name was Claire, and Adam knew her pretty well from all the times he came in.

"Claire," he said, "I know I have that rude girl with me again and I'm sorry. But I want you to do me a favor. She's going to try to order something with fish in it and I want you to tell her that you don't have any. No chicken either. Then if she asks for milk tell her you don't have any of that. You see, she's allergic to those foods and she tries to eat them even though they make her sick."

Claire gave him a shrewd glance. She wasn't as stupid as she looked.

"You're not just trying to make her mad, are you, Adam?"

He smiled. "Well, maybe. But if you do what I say I'll give you a big tip."

Claire laughed. "You kids. You kill me. Sure, whatever you want. I didn't like her anyway."

"I understand," Adam said.

He returned to his seat. Jessie was browsing through a math textbook and frowning.

"I don't understand any of this stuff," she said. "What are x and y?"

"They are unknowns in algebra. In most equations

you have to figure out what they are. In fact, you have to first figure out how to construct the equations, usually from a word problem." Adam took the book and skipped to a page where there were word problems. "Okay, say Farmer John has four horses. When he drives to town in his truck without towing his horses it takes him one hour. But if he takes his four horses the extra weight causes him to drive slower so he needs twenty minutes extra to get to town. Now how long will it take him to get to town if he brings only two horses?"

Jessie stared at him. "How am I supposed to know that?"

"That's what you have to figure out. You write it out as an equation." Adam picked up a pencil and began to scribble on a napkin in front of Jessie. "Okay, four horses slow down Farmer John twenty minutes. We can say that four x equals twenty."

"What is four x?" Jessie asked.

"The four horses."

"Why don't you call it four b?"

"It doesn't matter what you call it. But the most common symbols are x and y. What matters is that four of these things equal twenty minutes."

"I thought four of these things were equal to four horses? Now you are saying they are minutes."

"The problem is about how the horses relate to the minutes lost," Adam explained, pleased she was getting annoyed. "If four x equals twenty minutes, what does x equal?"

"I don't know. I don't care. I don't want to do this anymore."

"This is what you'll be doing all year, every night for five or six hours."

She was shocked. "You're kidding?"

"I told you algebra was hard. When school is on, you don't do anything but study."

"But what if you don't want to take algebra?"

Adam shook his head. "Then you've got to take calculus, which is a real killer. When you take calculus you don't even have the weekends free. You sleep and eat calculus," Adam lied.

Jessie was upset. "But we didn't used to have all these hard subjects."

Adam shrugged. "It's tough being a kid these days. And if you should flunk algebra, or any class for that matter, then they make you go to summer school. And that runs from six in the morning till ten at night—three months in a row."

Claire, their waitress, arrived. She had her pen and pad ready.

"May I take your order, please?" she asked.

Jessie grabbed the menu and quickly studied it. "Yes. I'll have your fish sandwich. Cooked lightly, no mayonnaise."

"I'm sorry," Claire said. "We have no fish sandwiches today."

Jessie was annoyed again. "Why not?"

Claire shrugged. "We just don't have any. What can I say?"

Jessie studied the menu some more. "Then I'll have your halibut steak. Cooked rare with no sauce."

Claire shook her head. "We're out of halibut."

Jessie blinked. "You're kidding?"

"I don't kid, miss. Is there something else you would like?"

"How about the swordfish?" Jessie asked.

"How about it?" Claire asked, clearly enjoying her role.

"Do you have it?" Jessie growled.

"Yes."

"I'll have it with—"

"But it's old," Claire interrupted. "We're about to throw it out."

Jessie looked ready to kill. "Are you saying you have no fish at all?"

"Yes."

"Why didn't you say that as soon as you walked up to the table?" Jessie yelled.

Claire smiled. "You didn't ask. May I get you something else?"

Jessie threw the menu down. "I'll have the chicken."

"I'm sorry, we just ran out of chicken five minutes ago."

Jessie was livid. "What do you have to eat then?"

Claire frowned. "Not much. Would you like a banana?"

Jessie turned to Adam. "I want to go somewhere else and eat."

"This is the best place in town," Adam said. "If they don't have fish or chicken here, you won't find it within a hundred miles of this town."

Jessie fumed. "I'll have a bowl of milk then."

"You can have the bowl," Claire said. "But we're out of milk as well."

"How can you be out of milk?" Jessie screamed.

Claire put her hands on her hips. "Really, young lady, if you're going to carry on like this I'm going to have to ask you to leave."

Jessie jumped up. "We are leaving. There's nothing here for me to eat."

Adam stood. "You're just going to have to learn to eat new things." He added, "Or else you're going to starve to death."

9

ADAM TOOK HER TO THE COMMUNITY SWIM-
ming pool next, the last place he figured Jessie would
want to go. He knew how much cats hated the water.
And Jessie did in fact look pretty miserable on the walk
over.

"You can't go to school unless you take PE," Adam
said. "And the only PE class offered this year is swimming."

Jessie was aghast. "For the whole year?"

"Yeah. We'll have to swim every morning for an
hour. And I've heard the pool at school is worse than
the community pool. It's not heated. In the winter you
have to break the ice before you can jump in."

Jessie was worried. "But I've never been able to swim. I've always been afraid of the water. Do we have to do this today?"

"Believe me, you want a lesson first. The swimming teacher will pick you up and throw you in the water. And if you try to get out of the pool before the hour is up, he'll grab you and hold you underwater until you turn blue. The guy is tough—he used to be a Navy SEAL."

Jessie shook her head. "I don't know if I can handle this."

Adam pointed her toward the girls' locker room. "You go in there and change. If you don't have a suit you can check one out. When you're through changing, meet me out at the water." He patted her on the shoulder and added, "Don't worry, I'll be with you every step of the way."

Looking miserable, Jessie went into the girls' locker room. Thinking he was doing a good job on her, Adam went into the boys' room and quickly got into a suit. A few minutes later he was waiting out by the water for Jessie to emerge. When she did, she kept glancing nervously at the water.

"Can we just start in the shallow end?" she asked.

"Sure. But we'll have to work our way into the deep end, if you really want to learn to swim."

"But I don't want to learn to swim. I told you that."

"Fine. But you'll probably drown in PE then. I heard a couple of kids drowned last year. But, like I said, it's a tough PE class."

Jessie was anxious. "Things sure weren't like this when I went to school."

"Times have changed, Jessie," Adam said.

They got in the water, in the shallow end, which was only two and a half feet deep. Just getting Jessie that far took all of Adam's persuasive abilities. Jessie treated the water as if it were boiling acid. But once she was in, and she saw the water was only up a little past her waist, she began to relax. But Adam didn't let her get too comfortable. He pulled her toward the deep end.

"The first day of PE," he said, "the teacher makes you jump off the diving board."

Jessie was horrified. "What? There's no way I'm doing that. I would sink right to the bottom. How deep does this pool get anyway?"

"Twelve feet. But you've got to do it today before you do it in PE."

She shook her head. "No way!"

Adam spoke in a reasonable voice. "We can jump off together. You can hold my hand. If you begin to sink I'll pull you up. I'm an excellent swimmer. You'll be in no danger, and once you get over your fear you'll be able to swim laps. You'll love it; you might even start training for the Olympics."

Jessie stared at him suspiciously. "Why are you making me do all this?"

Adam shrugged. "I'm just trying to help you out." He added, although it was forced, "Because I like you."

That pleased her. "Really?"

"Sure. I wouldn't say it unless I meant it."

"Do you think I'm cute?"

Adam had never told a girl that she was cute, especially one who had been a cat for the last couple hundred years. But for Sally, he felt he had to stretch his limits.

"Yeah," he said. "You're a kitty, I mean, a cutie."

She hugged him and beamed. "If it means that much to you, Adam, I'll go off the diving board with you."

But a minute later she wasn't so sure. Standing on the diving board beside him, she shook like, well, a cat that was about to be thrown into a swimming pool. She was holding on to him so tight he started to wonder if they were both going to drown. He had to untangle her arms from his.

"Just hold my hand," he said. "That's all you have to do."

She looked at him with her big green eyes.

"You promise not to let go?" she asked.

Of course that was exactly what he intended to do. He needed to scare her so bad that she'd want to be a cat again.

"Don't worry," he said, turning toward the water, four feet below them. "We'll jump on the count of three. One . . . two . . . three!"

In reality she did not jump. She must have lost her nerve at the last second, and he ended up pulling her off the diving board. The moment they hit the water, he let go of her hand. Even though she had stolen his friend's body and was a pain in the neck, he felt awful for betraying her trust in him. He knew how terrified she must be.

Jessie went straight to the bottom of the pool.

Paddling on the surface, Adam began to wonder what would happen to Sally if Jessie died. Big air bubbles were rising out of Jessie's mouth, and she could have only so much air in her lungs. Adam could see her frantically moving her arms and legs, and not going anywhere. He decided that enough was enough.

Adam took a deep breath and dove down.

He was not exaggerating when he had told Jessie what an excellent swimmer he was. In Kansas City, where he had grown up, he swam all the time in a lake near his home. In fact, there was a tall tree that hung out over the lake, which he jumped off. So he was used to diving deep.

But the moment he reached Jessie he knew he was in trouble.

She grabbed him. But not with a normal grip.

Jessie was strong, far stronger than he was. She was like one huge cat and her hands were like massive paws. She grabbed him so tight he couldn't move his arms, which wasn't good since he was trying to rescue her. Try as he might, he couldn't break free. Inches in front of him he could see that her face was turning blue from lack of oxygen. He understood that her strength was increased by her panic. He remembered a Red Cross instructor in Kansas City saying the first thing you had to learn when rescuing drowning people was not to give them a chance to drown you.

They were bobbing around near the bottom, but the moment Adam felt his feet really hit the floor of the pool, he pushed off with all his might. They rocketed toward the surface, and even broke free of it. But the ordeal was not over because he was still not free of her.

Because she was a girl—and he thought of himself as a protector of young women everywhere—he hated to hurt her, but he had to ram his knee up and into her gut. She loosened her grip on him and he was able to break loose. Quickly turning her over onto her back, he slipped his right arm around her neck and paddled them toward the side of the pool. Once there he forced her to put her hands on the ledge so he didn't have to hold her up. She was coughing and gagging and wasn't able to talk for a few minutes.

When she finally could speak, all she said was "Get me out of here."

Adam helped her out of the pool and pointed her in the direction of the girls' showers. He showered and dressed but he waited a long time before she reappeared. He expected her to come out all upset, either crying or mad at him. But when she emerged from the locker room, she was smiling as she had that morning. She walked over to him.

"That was fun," she said.

"Almost drowning was fun?"

She punched him. "Yeah. That was the worst thing that could happen to me. Now I've gotten over my fear. I think I am going to enjoy PE."

Adam nodded. "Okay." He had hoped the fright would be enough to end the day for her, at least as a human. He had nothing else planned. "What would you like to do now?"

She smiled. "I want to show you a cave."

"What cave?"

"It's not far from here. Just in the hills behind the cemetery." She paused. "Where you ran into Sally's cat yesterday."

Adam was cautious. "How do you know we ran into the cat there?"

"Sally told me."

"Sally told you a lot."

"Yeah. She told me all about you guys. I know you real well." She grabbed his arm. "Come on, you've been deciding what we're going to do all day. Now it's my turn."

Adam had no choice but to follow her. He still had to figure out a way to make her want to give up her human body. But he was beginning to wonder if his approach was all wrong. It had been Watch's plan, after all, and Watch hadn't even hung around to try to make it work. Briefly, he wondered how Watch and Cindy were getting along with Sally. He hoped Cindy had not taken Sally to the vet for shots.

Jessie had a thing about holding his hand that made Adam uncomfortable. Besides being shy about being seen in public so close to a girl, he was amazed by how tight Jessie could grip. He was reminded of when they had been on the bottom of the pool and she had almost drowned him. Yet she hadn't said anything to him about his kneeing her in the stomach, although he supposed he should apologize to her and explain why he did it. He didn't want her mad at him unless it was necessary.

They followed the path behind the cemetery that led into the hills. Adam tried making conversation, but Jessie seemed intent on getting to the cave. He tried to ask a couple of times what was there but she just smiled and said that he would see. Adam began to feel nervous. He'd had a bad experience the last time he had gone into a cave in Spooksville. It had taken him almost twenty-four hours to find his way back out.

The cave was behind a tree not far from the path where they had found the cat. But if Jessie had not led him straight to it he doubted if he would ever have seen it. From the outside, it appeared unremarkable. The opening was about as tall as a grown man, but the sides were narrow. He had to squeeze through to follow Jessie, and once he was inside he didn't want to go any farther.

"We don't have a flashlight," he said. "We can't walk too far from the entrance or we won't be able to see."

She offered her hand. "What I have to show you is only a little way inside."

He took her hand, reluctantly. "What is it?"

She smiled. "A body."

He let go of her hand in a hurry.

"What do you mean?" he gasped.

"There's a body chained in this cave. Don't worry, it's been dead a long time."

"Somehow that doesn't make me feel any better."

She continued to laugh. "It's not an old smelly body. It's a skeleton of a kid about our age." She stuck out her hand again. "Don't be such a coward."

If there was one thing Adam didn't like being called it was a coward. He took her hand, even though he didn't want to. He figured he would see the skeleton, maybe touch it once, and then get out of the cave as fast as possible. The place made him feel creepy like the cat had yesterday. Like Jessie did today.

They came to the skeleton a moment later.

She was right, the guy had been dead a long time.

His bones were as dry as kindling wood and were covered with a fine brown dust. His skull was completely hollow and his eye sockets were open holes, yet there was something about his face—something in his exposed jaw perhaps—that suggested life.

He was not lying in the cave but standing, chained to the wall by his wrists. Adam figured he had been alive when he had been locked in here. Jessie answered his unspoken question.

"He was chained in here by Madeline Templeton when he was only twelve and a half," she said. "That was two hundred years ago and she left him here to die of starvation. No one ever found out where Jack was."

"How do you know his name was Jack?" Adam asked, although he could make an educated guess, given that he knew Jessie was probably at least as old as the skeleton.

Jessie looked at him. In the dark her green eyes seemed much brighter. They peered at him like twin emeralds, dipped in radioactive liquid. All of a sudden Adam wished he were anywhere but in this dark cave standing next to this strange girl. It was almost as if she were trying to hypnotize him. He wondered if that was how Sally had been trapped by Jessie's evil spell.

"I just know," she said in a peculiar voice. There was almost a note of sorrow in her tone. Adam took a step back.

"I feel sorry for him," he said. "It must have been a horrible way to die."

Jessie nodded slowly. "Lots of people went searching for him. The whole town did. They even looked here, in this area, but they couldn't hear him screaming because Madeline had closed up the cave with bricks."

Jessie pointed to the floor. "You see the bricks are still here. The wall just collapsed the other day. But a little cement could fix it again."

Adam backed up another step. "Sounds like an interesting story. Why don't you tell me the rest of it while we walk back to town?"

Jessie suddenly stepped around him so that she was standing between him and the way out. She was fast; the move caught Adam by surprise.

"I would rather tell you the story in here," she said.

Adam swallowed. "I hope it's not a long story."

Jessie smiled sadly and her gaze was far away.

"There was a girl named Jessica," she said. "She liked this boy Jack, the same Jack you see hanging here. But they were just children, and it wasn't as if they were romantically involved or anything. Even though in those days people did get involved much younger. Anyway, Jessica had a friend named Madeline—she was a witch. Even when Madeline was young, she was so powerful that most people in town feared her. But Jessica didn't because she had grown up with Madeline. Jessica trusted her friend, especially when her friend promised to give her some of her power. In exchange Madeline said she only wanted a small favor. But what she didn't tell Jessica was that she liked Jack as well and didn't want to share him with anyone." Jessie paused and then suddenly rushed the ending as if it were too painful to spend time on. "So Madeline changed Jessica into a cat, and led Jack here by telling him Jessica was hurt. And then she chained him to the wall and left him to die." She stopped and Adam thought he saw a tear on her face. "It's a sad story, isn't it?"

"Why did Madeline kill Jack if she liked him?" he asked, curious.

Jessie sighed. "Because she realized too late that Jack would never like her the way he had liked Jessica. You see, Madeline was powerful but she was lonely as well. She was always using her power to win friends, but as a result none of her friends were real friends." Jessie paused. "With Jessica and Jack gone, Madeline had no one to talk to."

Adam tried to step past her. "We should tell the police about this body."

Jessie put a hand on his chest and stopped him. "No one's telling anyone about Jack."

Adam could feel how strong she was. "All right. We won't talk about Jack again."

He started to pass by her again. Again she stopped him.

"You know," she said.

"I know what?"

"Who I am."

He shrugged. "Sure. You're Jessie. Let's get out of here."

But she tightened her hold on his shirt. "This afternoon, the whole time, you were trying to discourage me from being a human. You made me do algebra, you wouldn't let me eat what I like, and then you tried to drown me."

"I saved you from drowning." He added quietly, "Anyway, you are human."

She kept staring at him. "I am now. But as you know I wasn't yesterday."

He forced a laugh. "What were you? A cat?"

It wasn't exactly the best example to use, he realized.

Jessie nodded faintly. "I was the black cat you found. The evil house-burning cat you were all afraid of. But like I said, you already know that. When I was getting dressed at the swimming pool, after you tortured me in the water, I realized that." She gripped his shirt tightly. "And I realized something else. You know what that was?"

Adam tried to back up but found he couldn't.

"No," he said.

Her voice was cold. "I realized you were not my friend. You were just pretending to be because you wanted to get something from me. You are like Madeline. She should have paid for what she did to me and Jack but she was too powerful. Even when I served her as a familiar, I could never take revenge on her. But I can take revenge on you!"

"Jessie—" Adam began.

But he wasn't given a chance to finish. Gripping his chest with ferocious strength—as if she were a lion—Jessie lifted him off the ground and pinned him to the wall beside Jack's skeleton. There was another set of chains pinned into the stone, and these she fastened around his wrists. But the handcuffs were old and rusty—the locking mechanism was shot. It didn't matter to Jessie. From the depths of her green eyes light blazed, like twin laser beams, and she fused the cuffs together. Adam was trapped. Jessie took a step back and grinned at him.

"I'll be back later with some cement," she promised. "I'll wall this place back up. Even if your friends come looking for you, even if you scream as loud as you can, no one will hear you." She pinched his cheek. "Good-bye, Adam. I really did think you were cute. You reminded me of Jack. And now—just think—you're going to look like him."

Jessie walked away.

Adam hung in the dark beside the skeleton of Jack.

He didn't know how he was going to get out of this mess.

10

MEANWHILE CINDY WAS FEEDING SALLY A chicken dinner. Sally seemed to enjoy it, but Cindy had to hold the drumstick for her if Sally was to get any meat off it. Cindy laughed as Sally growled when the drumstick was done. Cindy scratched the cat on the back of the head, which made Sally growl more.

"You can't have any more," Cindy said. "You don't want to be a fat cat. There's nothing more unattractive."

The cat tried to scratch Cindy's hand but Cindy was too fast for her. Cindy waved the drumstick at her.

"You don't want to make me mad," Cindy said. "Or you'll have no breakfast tomorrow."

"Careful," Watch advised. "Hopefully she won't be a

cat much longer," he said, checking one of his watches, "if Adam is successful with Jessie. Hey, he's been gone a long time."

They were sitting on what was left of Cindy's front porch, and it was getting late. The sun would set in an hour. Cindy left Sally alone for a moment and went over to sit beside Watch. He looked worried and she patted him on the back.

"Adam knows how to take care of himself," she said. "Even if he can't talk her back into being a cat, I don't think she can harm him."

Watch shook his head. "You forget that she's been a familiar for two centuries, and I doubt that she lost all her powers by becoming human. If she suspects Adam is trying to manipulate her, she could get really angry. Who knows what she might do to him?"

"Should we go look for him?" she asked.

Watch stood. "I think I'll look myself. I don't want to have to take the cat—I mean, Sally. She'd just slow me down. You stay here and watch her."

Cindy caught something odd in his tone. "You don't want me to come for another reason?"

Watch lowered his head. "I am thinking of going to the witch's castle, and asking her for help."

Cindy was concerned. "You know it's never a good

idea to push her. She said she told you all she was going to tell you. I don't want you going to that evil castle."

Watch looked up. "I got a lot of my eyesight back at that castle. I was going blind before I went there. I really don't think Ann Templeton is evil."

Cindy stood and touched his arm. "She may not be evil but she doesn't understand our idea of goodness. She's totally unpredictable."

Watch nodded. "But I'm afraid something is wrong with Adam. He should have at least called by now."

"The witch won't go out of her way to help Adam."

"She might. And I'm hoping Ann Templeton has some records about what happened back when Jessie was turned into a cat."

Cindy gave him a hug. "Go then. But what should I do if Jessie shows up here without Adam?"

"Be careful what you say to her."

When Watch reached the castle, he was surprised to find the moat torches burning. Usually the castle was dark and forbidding at evening time. But maybe Ann Templeton knew he was coming. He expected a goblin or troll to answer the door, but it was the witch herself. She was dressed in a long dark green robe and smiled when she saw who it was.

"Watch," she said. "You're just in time. Come in."

He stepped into the dark interior of the castle, which he knew from experience could change shape at a moment's notice. In the corner was a roaring fire, and not far from it was a long wooden table littered with old pieces of brown paper.

"Did you put the idea in my mind to come here?" he asked.

"Exactly." She led him toward the table and offered him a seat. "I am reviewing portions of Madeline Templeton's diary. As you can see it is not in good shape. I had to look long and hard to find what I have."

Watch sat down at the table. "You're going to all this trouble to help Sally?"

Ann Templeton smiled as she made herself comfortable across from him.

"Let's just say I have a curiosity about what happened with Madeline and this Jessie. If the information I find helps Sally, I don't mind. But I told you, I still think Sally will make a good cat. She should have been born with claws."

Watch nodded at the pieces of paper. "Does Madeline's diary discuss their relationship?"

"Yes. At first they were the best of friends. But then Madeline got jealous of Jessie's friendship with a boy. I think Madeline liked him as well."

"Is that when Madeline turned her into a cat?"

"Yes." Ann Templeton read one piece of old and cracked paper. "This entry was dated after Jessie was already a familiar. But even then Madeline seemed upset, but I think it had more to do with the boy." Ann Templeton suddenly frowned. "Oh, that wasn't very nice of her."

"What?" Watch asked.

"Madeline killed Jack. That was the name of the boy."

Watch swallowed. "Just because she was jealous?"

"Madeline had a terrible temper when she was young. She chained Jack in a cave not far from here, up behind the cemetery. Then she walled the entrance up." Ann Templeton set the page of the diary down. "He must still be there."

"But not in very good shape," Watch added.

Ann Templeton smiled faintly. "You know what I like about you, Watch?"

"I can't imagine."

"Even when things are at their darkest, you have a sense of humor. That's a good trait to possess, especially in this town."

"Thank you. It's a difficult town to grow up in, but an exciting one." He paused. "Why *does* so much weird stuff happen here? I've always wondered."

Ann Templeton laughed. "The answer to that question

would fill books. But I'll give you a hint. The answer lies in the stars and in the past and in the future."

"I don't understand."

"If I told you, it would ruin the mystery of Spooksville for you, and I won't do that. You have to discover the truth for yourself. But to do that you're going to have to look in all three places that I have described."

"Your daughter Mireen said your husband was from the star cluster the Pleiades." Watch paused. "Is Mireen around? I haven't talked to her in a while."

"She is busy with her studies. You may see her another time." She sharpened her tone. "And as far as my husband is concerned, I never speak of him. And you shouldn't either."

Watch nodded quickly. "I didn't mean to pry. I'm sorry."

Ann Templeton tapped the pages of the diary. "Something about this cave intrigues me. I feel there may be something there. Where did you find the cat yesterday?"

"Up behind the cemetery." He paused. "Near the cave, I suppose."

"Interesting. Jessica must have liked to stay close to Jack."

"You know Adam is supposed to be with Jessie now.

He's trying to show her that being a human isn't so great after all."

"Did he tell Jessie that he was onto her secret?"

"He didn't plan to tell her." Watch added, "But he's been gone a long time. I'm worried about him."

Ann Templeton paused and closed her eyes and put a hand to her head, near her forehead. For a moment she breathed funny, sort of rapidly. Then she became very still and Watch felt a strange power move through the room. Then she opened her eyes and stood.

"We will go up to this cave together," she said.

Watch jumped. "Now?"

"Not this minute. I have to speak to my trolls. Once a week I lecture them on good manners and civic responsibility. If I don't, they get all excited and want to burn and pillage the town. But we can go in half an hour. While you're waiting you can read in my library. I have many interesting books you might enjoy, a few even from the time of Atlantis and Lemuria."

"But is Adam at the cave? He might be in danger."

She laughed. "Adam enjoys a little danger."

11

CINDY WAS TRYING TO INTEREST SALLY IN A
can of tuna when there was a knock at the door. Cindy
hoped it was Adam as she hurried to the door. But when
she opened it, she froze solid. Jessie, her green eyes
blazing, stood on the burned porch.

"You seem surprised to see me," Jessie said. "May I
come in?"

Cindy glanced over her shoulder. The cat—Sally—had
come into the living room and was standing behind her now.

"N-now is not a good time," Cindy stuttered. "I have
company."

Jessie peered around. "I see you do. But that's all
right. I didn't want to come into your lousy house yes-

terday and I don't want to come into it this evening."
She paused and her face darkened. "I was just wondering
if you wanted me to take you to Adam."

"Where is he?"

"Come with me and I'll show you. Bring your cat; I
don't mind."

Cindy was worried. "What have you done to him?"

Jessie shrugged. "Nothing. He's perfectly well. I was
just on my way back to him. But then I got to thinking about you, and how much you like him. How you
would like to spend more time with him. And I thought
I should invite you along."

Cindy knew Jessie was up to no good but she felt
she had no choice but to follow her. Of course she suspected Jessie had somehow trapped Adam, and that
Jessie intended to capture her along with him. Jessie
clearly hated her, and obviously knew that Cindy knew
about her little black cat secret.

Cindy bent down and picked up Sally.

"All right, Jessie," she said. "We'll go with you."

"That's good." Jessie grinned. "You can help me carry
the cement."

As it grew dark outside, it became almost pitch-black in
the cave. Still Adam could make out some shapes. Not

that there was much to see. His aching arms and hands were already beginning to occupy most of his attention. Jessie had pinned them above his head, and his heart was having trouble pumping the blood to his fingertips. The cramping in his muscles was extraordinary. He wondered how long he could last before he would begin to cry out in pain. Of course he knew no one would hear him, with or without the brick wall. He wondered if Jessie really was coming back, or if she would wait until he was dead to wall him in. Neither alternative sounded pleasant.

Adam glanced around.

"I hate this place," he muttered.

"You get used to it," a soft voice replied.

Adam would have jumped out of his skin if he hadn't been chained.

"Who's there?" he gasped.

"Just me," the voice replied.

Adam had to take a breath. "Who is me?"

"Jack. I'm right here."

Adam blinked and stared at the skeleton on his right. He thought he noticed a faint movement.

"Jack," he whispered. "Are you Jack the skeleton?"

There was definite movement on his right. A bony hand raised up.

Adam did scream.

"Shh," Jack said. "Don't get excited. I know I've lost weight, but I'm not that bad looking."

Adam bit his lip and tried to catch his breath.

"You're alive?" Adam whispered.

"Sure. But I only wake up at night. What's your name?"

"Adam."

A bony hand brushed Adam's side and Adam screamed again.

"I just wanted to shake," Jack said, quickly withdrawing his bony fingers.

Adam was still trying to get a handle on the situation. A talking skeleton in a black cave was not his idea of fun company. He closed his eyes for a moment and took several long, deep breaths. When he opened his eyes again, Jack was still there, still staring at him with his empty eye sockets.

"Jack," Adam said carefully, "do you know you're a skeleton?"

Jack sounded offended. "Well, you'd be a skeleton, too, if you'd hung here as long as I have with nothing to eat."

Adam nodded, his heart still pounding in his chest.

"I understand that," he said. "But because you are a skeleton, you're not supposed to be alive."

Now Jack was definitely insulted. "Are you saying I should be dead? Is that what you mean?"

"Yes. Most skeletons are dead. All the ones I know about have been."

Jack sighed. "You don't like me. Here we're chained together in the same cave and you don't even want to be friends. You know it gets lonely in here without anyone to talk to."

"Jack," Adam said patiently. "My reaction to you has nothing to do with whether I like you or not. I'm just stunned that you can talk at all."

"Well, get over it then and we can talk about something. I haven't had anyone to talk to in a long time."

"How about Jessie?"

"What about her?"

"Hasn't she been coming to talk to you over the years?"

"No. She was a cat. Cats can't talk. You should know that."

"I suppose I should," Adam said dryly.

Jack continued. "Besides, she only knocked down the wall this morning. That was the first time I saw her as a human in I don't know how long. I did hear her purring outside the wall, if she happened by at night, which didn't happen too often. Usually she would come in the day when I couldn't move or talk."

"Why do you sleep during the day?"

"I don't know. I just got on a late schedule and found it hard to break."

"So what you're saying is that Jessie doesn't even know you're alive?"

"That's right. As a cat she couldn't break in here. I'm looking forward to talking to her." He paused. "I hope she doesn't mind that I'm not as handsome as I used to be. Do you think I'll have a problem there?"

Adam nodded reluctantly. "I'm afraid so, Jack. The girls I know are not really into dead people."

"But I'm not dead," Jack said briskly. "I thought I made that clear. I'm just malnourished. No offense, but you won't look much better if you hang around here long enough."

Adam sighed. "I guess. But I would like to get out of here. When Jessie returns can you talk her into letting me go?"

"I hope so. She used to be my friend. But I don't know how she's changed over the last two hundred years."

"I hate to say this, Jack, but she's not the nicest girl in the world. She stole my friend's body and turned her into a cat. She was the one who chained me here."

"Oh my," Jack said, shocked. "That doesn't sound like the Jessie I knew. I wonder why she changed so much?"

"Maybe it was being a cat so long."

"That's no excuse," Jack said. "I've been stuck in here all this time and I haven't lost my manners."

Adam frowned. "How did you pass the time?"

"I whistle to myself mainly. Would you like to hear me whistle? The more flesh you lose the better you can whistle. The air seems to blow through my whole body these days."

Adam heard a sound at the mouth of the cave.

"You can whistle for me later," Adam said. "I think someone's coming."

12

JESSIE APPEARED A MOMENT LATER, PUSH-
ing Cindy in front of her and holding a flashlight. Cindy
had her arms full. In one hand she carried the cat—
Sally—and in the other she had a bag of cement. The
cement looked heavy and Cindy appeared weary. But
when Cindy saw Adam chained to the wall, she dropped
both the cat and the cement and ran to his side.

"What has she done to you?" Cindy cried.

"Hung me up for decoration, I think," Adam said.

Cindy turned on Jessie. "You are a horrible creature!
You let him go this instant!"

Jessie laughed loudly. "You fool! No one is leaving
this cave except me. Even Sally, this old cat, is staying.

I'm going to wall you all in here and let you die in darkness."

Cindy stepped forward and tried to push her out of the way. But Jessie still had a cat's reflexes and struck Cindy across the face. The blow was strong, and Cindy landed in a heap at Adam's feet.

"Hey!" Adam shouted. "You don't have to get rough. We can talk about the situation."

Jessie sneered. "Talk about what? How I suffered the last two hundred years? How you tried to drown me the day after I finally freed myself? I trusted you, Adam, and you tried to trick me."

"I tried to trick you because you tricked Sally. You stole her body."

The cat growled angrily.

"I deserve a human body!" Jessie snapped. "I earned it!"

"Right," Adam said sarcastically. "You earned the right to torture and kill people. What if Jack was here today? What would he say about his sweet Jessie?"

Jessie strode right up to Adam and drew her hand back to slap him. She almost stepped on Cindy, who was slowly regaining her wits and sitting up.

"Don't talk about Jack!" Jessie cried. "Jack belonged to me! If he was here now he'd understand what I've gone through! He wouldn't blame me!"

There was a long pause.

Adam hoped Jack would say something soon.

He had set the situation up for Jack to speak.

"I don't understand why you are hurting these people," Jack said softly.

Jessie leapt back as if she had been shot. Her head twisted left and right. Her breath came in a sharp pant. In the light of her flashlight, her skin was the color of snow.

"Who's there?" she demanded.

The skeleton moved slightly. "It's me. It's Jack."

Jessie put a hand to her horrified face and backed into the wall of the cave. "No!" she cried. "It can't be! You died two hundred years ago!"

Jack lifted a bony arm and his skull rocked to the side. He seemed to be looking down at his own hand. Adam understood he hadn't had any light to see himself in all this time.

"I admit I don't look too good," Jack said quietly. "But as I was telling Adam here, I'm not dead. You just don't get much to eat walled up in a black cave. But I'm not the main issue here. I'm concerned about you, Jessie. You seem to have gotten as bad tempered as Madeline."

Jessie stared at him as if in disbelief. But she recovered remarkably fast and it must have been her training as a familiar. "Madeline was the one who locked you in here. How can you call her something as simple as bad tempered?"

"Because I've forgiven her," Jack said simply. "I've had a lot of time to think and forgive. I suggest you do the same, especially now that you have your body back. Really, Jessie, you don't have much to complain about. You've still got your figure while mine has gone to pieces."

"Literally," Adam muttered.

Jessie shook her head. "No. I can't let it go. I suffered so long."

"I suffered, too," Jack said. "At least as much as you. But it won't ease either of our suffering to hurt other people. Now let Adam go and help this nice girl up and give that cat back her human body. Then maybe we can talk about old times."

Jessie was stunned. "You won't talk to me unless I do these things?"

The skeleton shook his bony head. "No. You are wrong here and you know it. So Madeline harmed us? We don't have to follow her example."

Jessie was not convinced. Apparently her bitterness went deep.

"But I want my life back!" she complained. "It was stolen from me and I deserve it back!"

"You can have a life," a voice said from the direction of the entrance. "But not the one you have stolen."

Adam stared in amazement as Ann Templeton and Watch stepped into the cave. The witch wore a long black coat and carried in her right hand a green jewel that lit the way better than any flashlight. Watch hung close to her as if they were old friends. Ann Templeton surveyed the scene and then offered Cindy a hand and helped her to her feet. Cindy brushed off her pants and retreated to the wall closest to Adam, who was still stuck to the wall.

"Thank you," Cindy muttered to Ann Templeton, although she continued to watch the witch and Jessie with fear.

Ann Templeton nodded and turned to Jessie.

"I am sorry for what Madeline did to you," the witch said. "I have just come from my castle. I have been reading her diary. I know that Madeline had a temper and that she acted rashly in regard to you and Jack. On her behalf, I ask for your forgiveness."

Jessie stared at her. "You look like her."

Ann Templeton nodded. "Except I have dark hair and she had red hair. Do you accept my apology?"

"I do," Jack said brightly.

But Jessie slowly shook her head.

"I will accept it when you give Jack back his body," she said. "Not until then."

"Now that sounds like a good idea," Jack said.

But Ann Templeton shook her head. "Madeline cast this spell. I cannot fully reverse it. If I am to restore Sally to her normal body, I cannot create two new human bodies. That would be beyond my powers. But I can create an extra cat body if you wish, for Jack."

"I have always liked Siamese cats," Jack remarked.

Jessie was confused. "What are you saying?"

"Isn't it clear?" Ann Templeton said. "You are free to leave here with Jack. But as cats, not people. You have to give Sally back the body you stole from her."

"Madeline stole my body!" Jessie said bitterly.

"Yes, she did," Ann Templeton said patiently. "But that was long ago. This is now. You have these choices, none other."

Jessie considered. "If I want, I can leave here? In this body?"

"I won't stop you," Ann Templeton said. "And I don't think anybody else here would be capable of stopping you."

"But I might try," Watch muttered.

Jessie played with her hair, her thoughts far away. "I could stay human."

"But then you would begin to age," Ann Templeton warned. "But as a cat, both of you can be made immortal. If that's what you want."

"I like all the things cats do," Jack mused. "Chicken, all kinds of fish . . ."

"Quiet, Jack," Jessie said. "I'm thinking."

"You might want to think about Jack while you're deciding," Adam suggested.

Jessie jerked her head up and stared at the skeleton. "Has it been hard for you, too?" she asked in a gentle voice.

Jack sighed. "You know I don't like to complain, but, yeah, it's been lonely hanging all by myself in this cave for two hundred years. I'd like to get outside and stretch, even if it's in a cat's body. At least everybody wouldn't be looking at my bones like right now." He paused. "We can have fun together, Jessie. It might even be like old times."

Jessie smiled faintly. "Do you remember the old times, Jack?"

"Sure I do," he said. "I remember that you were always the one to think of other people first."

Jessie shook her head. "No. That was you."

Jack nodded his head. "Both of us were good people. And these seem like good people, too. Don't hurt them, Jessie, not when you don't have to."

Jessie finally broke into a real smile. "All right, Jack, for you I will give up being a girl. Just don't ask me to chase after birds with you. I got tired of that a century ago."

"We'll just chase squirrels," Jack promised.

Jessie turned to Adam. "Is algebra really that bad?"

"It can be pretty bad," Adam said. "Unless you're as smart as Watch."

"Or you have last year's test papers," Watch said, kidding.

Jessie laughed and turned back to Ann Templeton.

"I accept your apology," she said. "But make me a white cat this time. Please?"

"And me a Siamese," Jack added.

Ann Templeton raised her magical green stone.

"Everybody close your eyes," she said. "This is a magical moment."

They did as she asked.

And a great power filled the cave.

Then they heard a voice in the midst of the magic.

A complaining voice.

"Cindy," Sally said. "I wanted the rest of that chicken. And I think you knew that."

TURN THE PAGE FOR A SNEAK PEEK AT
SPOOKSVILLE #11: THE DEADLY PAST

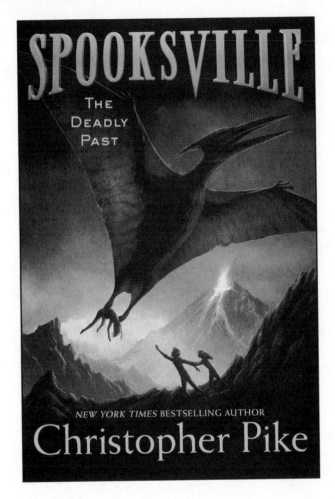

THE HORROR STARTED WITHOUT WARNING.

Adam Freeman and his friends were not far from home when they were attacked, just a half mile north of Spooksville, in an area where they seldom went. The woods they had hiked through to get there were not nearly so thick as the others around Spooksville. Resting on top of a hill, they saw nothing but rocks, desolate valleys, and a few bushes. Sally Wilcox, who had led them to the spot, said it looked like the far side of the moon.

"I bet they used to do nuclear testing here," she said as they continued climbing to the top of a rocky bluff that gave them a view of the ocean and Spooksville itself. "That's why not much grows here."

"That's ridiculous," Cindy Makey replied, brushing her long blond hair back from her cute face. "The government only performs nuclear tests in Nevada."

Sally stared hard at her with brown eyes that matched her brown hair. "I wasn't talking about the U.S. government," she said. "Remember Spooksville used to be part of ancient Lemuria, which went under the Pacific Ocean more than twenty thousand years ago. New Agers believe the Lemurian culture was peaceful, but I know for a fact that they built just as many bombs as we have today."

"Like you would know," Cindy snapped.

"Bum does say that Lemuria really existed," Watch said tactfully. Watch was known for always wearing four watches and having no last name.

"I hate to disagree with Bum," Adam Freeman said, catching his breath and wiping the sweat from his face. Adam was the shortest one in the group, and very conscious of the fact. Yet he was also the group's leader. "But how come there isn't more evidence of Lemuria and Atlantis still lying around?"

"You heard what Bum said," Watch replied. "When the two lands warred, they completely wiped each other out. But Bum says that Lemuria and Atlantis were descendants of even more ancient cultures. I believe him. I think our history books are very limited in their scope."

"But do you really think this place used to be radio-active?" Cindy asked, uneasily glancing around. "If that's true, we shouldn't be here."

"Why?" Sally asked with a snigger. "Are you afraid you might mutate into a plain-looking girl?"

"It looks like that happened to you already," Cindy replied.

Watch raised his hand before the two girls could get going. "If there was radiation here," he said, "there would be no plant life at all. I don't think we have to worry about it."

Adam cocked his head to one side. "What's that funny sound?"

"I don't hear anything," Sally said before pausing to listen closely. Then a puzzled expression crossed her face. "It sounds like wind blowing through a narrow valley."

Watch shook his head, as he also listened. "It sounds like a distant heartbeat to me." He scanned the area with his thick glasses. "But I don't see anything that could be making the sound. Do you guys?"

Cindy pointed. "What about that bird way over there?"

The brown bird to which Cindy was pointing seemed to be flying over a mountain range far beyond Spooksville. This puzzled Adam who didn't understand how they could even see something as small as a bird at such a distance. The sharp peaks over which the bird swept were at least three miles away. Also, it was kind of a funny-looking bird, with a long pointed head and an especially wide wingspan. He shook his head as he stared at the creature.

"That can't be a bird," he said.

"Of course it's a bird," Sally said impatiently. "What else could it be? A plane?"

Watch—who didn't see very well even wearing his glasses—stared at the strange creature. "I think Adam is right," he said after a long pause. "That's much too big to be a bird."

Sally shielded her eyes from the glare of the sun. "How can you tell how big it is?" she asked. "It's so far away."

"That's our point," Adam said. "We shouldn't be able to see it from here."

The brown bird appeared to see them.

It turned in their direction. The peculiar sound grew louder.

"Whatever it is, it's definitely making the sound," Watch said. "And look how fast it's coming. Now it's twice as big as it was a minute ago."

Sally was getting worried. "No bird can fly that fast."

"So it can't be a bird," Cindy insisted.

Adam began to back up. "Let's argue about what it is later. Right now it's coming our way at high speed and it's big. I think we should take cover."

Sally slowly nodded. "It might be hungry."

Cindy giggled uneasily. "We're going to feel stupid running from a bird."

Watch had also begun to back up. "I would rather feel stupid than dead." He paused and squinted. The bird—or whatever it was—let out a screeching cry. It pulled in its wings and seemed to go into free fall, plunging toward them like a missile. Even Watch, who seldom showed any sign of fear, stammered as he spoke next. "That looks like a pterodactyl."

"What's that?" Cindy asked.

Sally gasped. "A dinosaur!"

Watch shook his head. "It's not technically a dinosaur. But it lived at the time of dinosaurs, and was just as deadly."

"But that's impossible!" Cindy cried.

"Nothing is impossible in this town!" Adam yelled. He grabbed Cindy by the arm and began to pull her backward. "Let's get out of here. Now!"

They half-ran and half-slid down the bluff into a

narrow valley. But then they became terribly confused. They each began to run in a separate direction, having no idea where to go. Adam stopped them.

"We have to find a cave!" he yelled.

"We passed one a few minutes ago," Sally cried, stopping, pointing. "It was back that way!"

Watch pointed in the opposite direction. "I thought it was that way. But we'll never make it that far. We have to find something closer."

They searched the area anxiously.

The pterodactyl screeched again. Now its leathery wings were clearly visible, as well as its huge mouth. The monster seemed to be coming at them at a hundred miles an hour. It would be on them in seconds. Already the creature was flexing its sharp claws. Adam knew they had to get out of the open.

"If we can find a rock overhang," Adam said, "it could stop the pterodactyl from swooping in and snatching one of us."

"No!" Sally protested. "We need a cave to be safe!"

Watch grabbed her arm this time. "Adam is right! We'll never make it back to that cave! There's an overhang! Let's go to it!"

They took off for the far end of the narrow valley, which dead-ended at a wall with a sharp overhang that jutted twenty feet out from it. Unfortunately, the over-hang would be at least twenty feet over their heads. So it afforded little protection. As a group they pressed themselves against the limestone wall.

"I wish I had a hand laser," Watch said, staring up at the approaching monster.

"A strong stick might help," Adam said, spying one halfway up the side of the stone wall. He pointed. "I'll try for it."

The pterodactyl screeched a third time.

It was maybe five seconds away.

Sally grabbed Adam's arm and pulled him back against the wall. "Stay here, you nut!" she cried. "It'll kill you!"

Adam shook her off. "It will kill us all if we don't frighten it away." Glancing up at the pterodactyl once, he braced himself and then leapt toward the stick. The monster bird had incredible control of its seemingly wild plunge. It immediately veered toward Adam, who was just putting his hand on the stick. Suddenly the pterodactyl extended its massive wingspan, which was at least twenty feet across, to slow itself enough to grab Adam. Even so it was still traveling at high speed, and that may have been what saved Adam.

The creature tried to grab him but missed.

Sort of. The claw scraped Adam's right shoulder. Adam felt a wave of searing pain.

Blood stained his shirt.

"Adam!" the others screamed.

The pterodactyl was making another pass at him. This time Adam could smell it—like a cloud of rotting vegetation—blowing over him. The creature was not coming so fast this time, but rather, seemed to be plotting its moves. Adam could see the hungry intelligence in its huge black and red eyes. Red saliva dripped from its mouth, and Adam wondered what it had eaten last, if it had been human.

"Get back here!" Watch yelled.

Yet even though Adam was in pain and bleeding, he still wanted the stick. He understood that they needed it in order to beat back the pterodactyl to reach real shelter. The overhang would not discourage the creature for long. It could always land, and peck at them with its long beak.

"Coming!" Adam shouted as he grabbed the stick. His wound was serious. Blood dripped on the ground in front of him as he bent over. But with the long hard stick in his hand he felt a wave of confidence. The pterodactyl wasn't going to scratch him again!

Too bad the monster didn't share his conviction.

The pterodactyl swept in again, its wide wings stirring up eye-stinging dust. In spite of its great size, the creature was remarkably agile. It must have been smart as well, because seeing Adam's stick, it went for that first. With one swipe of the monster's claws, Adam almost had his hard-won weapon ripped from his hand. Quickly Adam adjusted his strategy. He started swinging the stick frantically, rather than hoping to land one solid blow.

"Take that, you overgrown chicken!" he shouted as he struck at the pterodactyl. By chance, one blow caught the flying reptile on the top of the head and the thing let out a bloodcurdling scream.

"Kill it!" Cindy yelled from beneath the overhang.

"The pterodactyl probably thinks you're talking to him!" Sally shouted at him. "Get over here, Adam! Quit being such a hero!"

"You guys get to the cave!" he shouted back. "I'll keep it busy!"

"We're not leaving you!" Sally hollered. She turned to Watch and asked, "Should we leave him?"

Watch hesitated. "I hate to, but maybe we should. It could come after us any second, and we have only one stick."

"I'm not going to leave Adam," Cindy said firmly.

Just then the pterodactyl made another grab for Adam. He saw it coming, but it didn't help much. This time the birdlike creature used its wings as well as its claws. Adam was knocked to the ground and for a moment lost his grip on the stick. The pterodactyl was indeed smart and immediately went for the stick. It was only Watch's quick thinking that prevented them from losing their only weapon. Watch grabbed the stick before the pterodactyl could, and swung at the creature's legs, making contact. Again the pterodactyl screamed and flapped higher above them. Watch helped Adam up.

"I think I hurt it," Watch said. "Now's the time to make a run for it."

Adam nodded. "I'm game!"

They raced toward the cave they had spotted. The monster seemed prepared to let them go. It flew high into the air and appeared to search around for an easier meal. But none of them let it out of their sight. Indeed, they all had trouble running because they kept looking over their shoulders. Watch continued to hold on to the stick.

"I wish we could find another one of these," he said. "Even if we reach the cave, we won't be safe. The pterodactyl could always squeeze its way in."

"Maybe there'll be another stick near the cave," Adam gasped, his shoulder still bleeding. In fact, running was making it bleed even more. He desperately needed a few minutes to stop, put pressure on the wound, and catch his breath. But he was willing to run until he bled to death. Just the thought of the pterodactyl carrying him to its nest filled him with the strength to go on.

"I have my lighter," Sally said, struggling to catch her breath with the rest of them. "If we build a fire, we could drive it off for good."

Watch glanced over his shoulder again. "It's still observing us."

"What does it want?" Cindy cried, probably more scared than any of them.

"It wants to eat us," Sally said grimly. "It will probably chew on our brains first and then begin to munch on our small intestines."

"I am so glad we have you here to tell us in what order it will eat us," Adam said.

Sally was concerned about Adam. Even as she ran, she reached over and tried to check on his wound. "You need a big bandage," she said.

"Right now I'd rather have a big shotgun," Adam replied.

The cave was only a hundred yards up ahead when

the pterodactyl attacked again. They were caught off guard because the monster had momentarily disappeared over the rim of the valley through which they were running. They had taken its disappearance to mean it was leaving them. But then suddenly it appeared in front of them. Even though they all saw it, it was flying so fast that Watch didn't have time to bring up the stick.

Claws extended, the pterodactyl swept over Sally.

She was lifted off the ground.

The others screamed.

Sally, moving faster than she had ever moved in her life, leaned over and bit the pterodactyl's toes. The monster howled in pain and dropped Sally.

She rolled through about ten tumbles before she came to a halt.

The others ran to her.

"Are you all right?" Cindy cried as Adam and Watch helped Sally up.

"Yes," Sally said in a calm voice as she brushed off her clothes. "None of my bones are broken and my brain is uninjured." But then she began to shake visibly and had to put a hand to her mouth to stop herself from moaning. "That dinosaur tastes awful," she whispered.

Adam pointed toward the sky. "It's coming again.

Watch, give me the stick. I think I know how to fight him off."

"Better you than me," Watch agreed, handing over the stick. "We'll keep heading for the cave."

But they weren't given a chance to head anywhere. The pterodactyl was obviously mad that his dinner had got away again. It attacked again once more, using its wings as its weapon. Adam swung at it with the stick while the others began to pelt it with rocks but the thing was simply too big and too fast to be stopped by such a defense. Plus the sound coming out of its toothy mouth was terrifying. It kept squawking as if they didn't quit fighting back and hand over one of them to eat, it would eat them all.

Then an amazing thing happened.

Watch managed to throw a rock so perfectly that it went down the pterodactyl's throat. There was no mistaking what happened next. The creature began to choke. Indeed, its struggle for air was so intense that it had to stop flapping its wings and land.

"This is our chance!" Adam cried. "Head for the cave!"

They took off for the dark opening.

Behind them the pterodactyl continued to gag.

The interior of the cave was dark and cool. It was a shame the opening wasn't narrow, to keep out large monsters. Watch believed it was wide enough to allow the pterodactyl inside, and for that reason they needed a fire. If they had learned one thing about the pterodactyl, they knew it didn't give up easily.

"But we've got nothing in here that will burn," Sally complained as she searched the dusty floor of the cave.

"That's not true," Watch said. "We've got the stick and we've got our clothes. If we wrap pieces of cloth around the stick we might be able to discourage the pterodactyl so that it leaves us alone."

Adam began to pull off his shirt. "Good idea. Take mine."

Sally shook her head. "Yours is too bloody. Watch, give me your shirt." Sally pulled out her Bic lighter, which she always carried no matter what. Watch quickly pulled off his shirt and the two of them began to tie it to the stick while Adam held on to the branch. Cindy was by the door of the cave, watching the pterodactyl.

"Hurry!" Cindy yelled. "It's coughed up the rock!"

The pterodactyl had recovered. But rather than fly toward the cave, it slowly began to walk in their direction. Perhaps it thought it had them cornered. The sight of the bird monster walking was even more disturbing than its flying and swooping in for an attack. Cindy began to freak out.

"We're trapped in here!" she cried.

"We're not trapped," Sally said as she touched the flame of the lighter to Watch's shirt. "But this shirt isn't going to burn very long. Cindy, give me your blouse."

Cindy stopped freaking out and looked embarrassed. "No. You burn your blouse first."

"My blouse is brand-new and cost twenty dollars for your information!" Sally snapped. "Besides, I am by nature more shy than you."

"I think the dinosaur is more shy than you," Cindy said.

"Give me the stupid stick and quit arguing!" Adam said as Watch's shirt began to catch fire. "I've got to scare it away!"

Adam pulled the stick away from Sally and hurried toward the cave entrance. He was just in time to meet the pterodactyl head on. To Adam's relief the monster recoiled from the flames. But once again Adam was struck by how smart the creature was. It seemed to know that the shirt could not burn long before going out. It withdrew several paces but didn't fly away. Beside Adam, Cindy began to panic again.

"It's not fooled!" she moaned.

Adam was grim. "It doesn't matter how many clothes we burn. It'll wait for us."

Watch moved up beside them. "I've checked, this cave doesn't go back too far. It doesn't even narrow."

Sally also joined them. "What if we draw straws or something?"

Cindy was horrified. "You mean sacrifice one of us so the others can get away?"

Sally shrugged. "I think it will better that it doesn't get us all. While the thing is eating one of us, the other three can get away."

"Would you stop talking about its eating us!" Cindy screamed.

"Well, it ain't going to play catch with us!" Sally screamed back. "We have to face facts!"

"We're not sacrificing anybody!" Adam snapped, still holding the burning stick. "We need to come up with a better defense. Watch, you always have good ideas. Can you think of anything?"

Watch sighed. "No. And I've been racking my brain. There might be a dozen things that could drive it off, but unfortunately they're all back in town." He paused. "Let me take the stick. I'll try to keep it occupied while you guys try to make it to town."

Adam shook his head. "No way. You wouldn't last long."

"You offered to do it," Watch said.

"That was just to give you time to make it to the cave," Adam said. "How about if we try for another cave? A tighter one that the pterodactyl can't fit into?"

Watch shook his head. "I know this area better than you, and I can't think of another cave that's even close."

The flames from Watch's shirt began to flicker.

The pterodactyl took a step closer, saliva dripping out of its mouth.

"It's going out!" Cindy cried.

Adam felt desperate. "Is there any way we can block off the entrance of the cave?"

"With what?" Sally demanded. "Our dead bodies?"

"We are not going to die," Adam snapped at her. "Sally, Cindy—you two get to the rear of the cave. Watch and I will try to hold it off with the stick."

Neither of the girls protested. The sight of the pterodactyl slowly approaching on its long nailed feet was enough to shatter the strongest will. Even Adam and Watch began to back up, without consciously realizing it. The pterodactyl's huge eyes seemed to swell in anticipation. It knew it had them, that there was no escape for the frail humans.

"If only this stick was sharp at one end," Adam said bitterly. "We could stab it, make it think twice about attacking again."

"We don't have time to sharpen it," Watch said quietly.

Adam glanced over at him. "Is this it? Is this the end?"

Watch took a deep breath. "Maybe not for all of us. But it will take one of us, that's for sure."

"And that one will die?"

"Yes. Horribly."

Adam grimaced. "It can't be one of the girls."

"It can't be one of us." Watch paused. "You are brave, Adam. But even you cannot just walk in front of that beast and let it take you. No one could."

The pterodactyl skipped toward them.

The flames at the end of the stick died.

The pterodactyl stuck its head in the mouth of the cave and screeched.

"Stop it!" Cindy screamed behind them.

Adam swung weakly with the stick. "It can't get any worse than this," he gasped.

Watch put a reassuring hand on Adam's uninjured shoulder. "But this might be the perfect chance to get a good shot at it. Maybe if you went for one of its eyes, partially blind it. That could be our only hope. Aim for an eye."

Adam nodded. "I'll try."

He did try, but his effort proved useless. The pterodactyl was too quick for him, and the beast knew instinctively how to protect its eyes. It held its head back as it advanced, using its claws to lead its attack. Several times Adam almost had his stick ripped from his hands.

Each step backward brought Adam and Watch closer to the rear of the cave, to the girls, and to the end of the line. In all the bizarre dangers Adam had faced since moving to Spooksville, he had never felt so helpless.

"I have an idea," Sally said behind Adam as he neared the rear wall. "Let's wrap another piece of cloth around the stick, set it on fire, and then crack open my lighter and douse it with what fluid is left in the container. That will create one huge flame that should last a few seconds. While it's burning, Adam, try to get the end of the stick into the thing's mouth. If that doesn't chase it away, we might be able to slip past the beast to get outside."

"We'll be easy pickings outside," Watch said. "Especially with no stick to protect us."

The pterodactyl raised a claw and swiped at them.

Adam and Watch jumped all the way back.

The four of them pushed up against the back wall of the cave.

"We are practically dessert in here!" Sally shouted. "Let's do it! Rip off the dry part of your shirt, Adam! Now!"

Adam did as he was told. In seconds Sally had the

cloth wrapped around the end of the stick. First she lit the cloth and then cracked open the lighter by smashing the top of it against the cave wall. Adam had to hold the tip of the burning stick close to her, and as a result the pterodactyl was free to approach within ten feet. Sally held the open lighter fluid container not far from the burning cloth.

"When I throw this liquid on the end," she said, "there will be a burst of fire. But you'll have to move fast, Adam. Understood?"

"I understand," Adam said. "But we have to be clear about what we're doing. If we're just trying to get outside, then we'll be lucky to create a crack where we can slip by the beast. We will have to go one at a time, in order. Cindy, you go first. Then Sally and Watch. I'll follow you guys out."

"That's okay with me," Sally said eagerly, nervously eyeing the pterodactyl. "Let's do this on the count of three. One . . . Two . . . Three!"

Sally threw the fluid on the fire.

The end of the stick exploded in flames.

Adam thrust the stick at the pterodactyl just as the creature leaned forward to take a bite out of one of them. The pterodactyl had its mouth open. Adam got the end of the stick past its teeth and tongue and partway down its throat. The pterodactyl let out a deafening screech of pain and bent its narrow beak down as it tried to be rid of the fire. The stick just flew out of Adam's hands. He didn't even have a chance to react.

But the uproar created the opening they needed to get outside.

Cindy shoved by Sally and dashed past the creature. Sally followed closely, with Watch and Adam bringing up the rear. Within five seconds of attacking the pterodactyl they were back outside in the fresh air. For a moment they all felt incredible relief. But then the monster screamed from the depths of the cave and they understood that it was far from defeated.

"Run!" Adam shouted.

"Where?" Sally shouted back.

"Anywhere!" Watch said.

So they ran, back the way they had come, back up to the bluff where they had first seen the pterodactyl. But the exercise was no solution. They were dealing with an enemy that was twenty times bigger and stronger than they were. One that was used to killing to live. Really, it had been hopeless from the start.

They were almost to the bluff that overlooked Spooksville and the ocean when the pterodactyl appeared in the sky once more. It rose directly above them, higher and higher, and for a few seconds it seemed that it would keep going into the wild blue yonder and they would be safe. But then it began to arc downward, tucking in its massive wings and pointing its ugly head toward the ground. Once more it raced toward them like a deadly missile, a blur of brown death. And all the while it screeched, a horrible sound of revenge. They had hurt it and now it wanted to hurt them.

They could only stand, frozen, and watch it come.

There was only one question in their minds.

Which one of them would it take?

At the last instant the pterodactyl spread its huge wings.

A wave of foul odor and sweeping air passed over them, as well as a dark shadow. Cindy screamed, maybe they all did. But it was Cindy who screamed the loudest because the pterodactyl had chosen her to be its victim. One moment she was standing beside Adam and staring at the horror in the sky. The next she was being dragged kicking and screaming into the air. Now she was a part of the horror, and as the pterodactyl flew off to the distant peaks, it seemed as if they could hear her screaming still. Yet they all knew that was impossible.

Adam bowed his head. They all did.

Their friend was gone.

About the Author

CHRISTOPHER PIKE is the author of more than forty teen thrillers, including the Thirst, Remember Me, and Chain Letter series. Pike currently lives in Santa Barbara, where it is rumored he never leaves his house. But he can be found online at ChristopherPikeBooks.com.